**"Why don't you stay
here with me, Dani?"**

Dani's eyes widened incredulously as
they searched his face to catch a
trace of humor. There was none.

"What do you think I am?" she asked
thickly. "Even if I were up for grabs,
there's nothing about you that would
interest me, Burt."

"No? That's not the impression I got
yesterday." His hand touched her
face, his fingers brushing lightly over
her cheek and across her parted lips.

She flushed. "Well, I'm not about to
be used by you because you
h-haven't seen a woman in a while!"

A flicker of his dark eyes showed that
he had taken her meaning, but it
obviously made no dent in his
maddeningly arrogant assurance.

"What is there to stop me from doing
whatever I like with you?"

ELIZABETH GRAHAM
is also the author of this

Harlequin Presents

392—DANGEROUS TIDE

and these
Harlequin Romances

Many of these titles are available at your local bookseller.

For a free catalogue listing all available Harlequin Romances
and Harlequin Presents, send your name and address to:

HARLEQUIN READER SERVICE,
M.P.O. Box 707, Niagara Falls, NY 14302
Canadian address: Stratford, Ontario N5A 6W2

ELIZABETH GRAHAM

thief of copper canyon

Harlequin Books

TORONTO • LONDON • LOS ANGELES • AMSTERDAM
SYDNEY • HAMBURG • PARIS • STOCKHOLM • ATHENS • TOKYO

Harlequin Presents edition published January 1981
ISBN 0-373-10403-0

Original hardcover edition published in 1980
by Mills & Boon Limited under the title
King of Copper Canyon

CHAPTER ONE

"DANI, HONEY, I wish you wouldn't go rushing off like this. You've never been to Canada in your life, yet here you are planning to travel over a thousand miles to get there all by yourself."

Her mother's words were still echoing in Dani Benson's mind long after she had left the environs of Los Angeles far behind. Not even the sight of Northern California's stands of mighty redwoods had the power to obliterate her sense of frustration over the way her life had been shaping up lately. And not just her own life, she reminded herself grimly as she guided her blue gray sports car—a gift from a grateful auto dealer for her part in promoting his products—through the towering trees on both sides of the highway.

Marsha Benson, Dani's mother, seemed to deteriorate daily in the health to which she had valiantly tried to cling after being stricken with the muscular disease that now kept her confined to the wheelchair she and Dani had managed to buy from their dwindling finances. Marsha needed a course of treatments that, although they wouldn't cure her, would go a long way toward alleviating some of the pain that constantly racked her. Treatments that were as far out of their reach as the moon.

But it didn't have to be that way, Dani reflected in the plastic confines of her motel room that night. That was her main reason for leaving all that was familiar to her. The letter that had come two weeks earlier telling of her grandfather's death in British Columbia, Canada, had said nothing about an inheritance for his sole remaining relatives. But Dani knew that Henry Benson, a migrant American, had been a man of substance in those parts, owning a ranch extending to several thousand acres, and with an appropriate number of cattle to go with those acres. And where there were cows, there must be money. Money that could be used to provide the treatment Marsha needed.

It had come as no surprise that Henry Benson had left no will. He had been a wanderer from the time of his wife's death when Dani's father, Daniel, had been a boy. Daniel Benson had been brought up by an obscure aunt in California, one who had encouraged his literary ambitions but barely lived to see the first of a string of minor motion-picture screenplays he wrote. The flat fees paid to him for his efforts had been sufficient to keep their small family in reasonable comfort, but on his death two years ago Dani and her mother had been left almost destitute. Dani had been forced to abandon her plans for a university education and had turned instead to the only offer open to her. Fortunately, her fresh, innocent beauty was in vogue at that time, and she was snapped up by a modeling agency that exploited her marketable charms and kept her reasonably solvent.

A frown marred the smooth area of her forehead. If only Emory Harden, head of the agency, hadn't said all those things to her three days ago!

"Innocent is out now, baby," he had told her in his nasal tones. "What advertisers want now is the sexy look, girls who look as if they know what life is all about."

"And what makes you think I don't?" Dani had flared.

"Come on, Dani, you have innocence written all over you." Emory's eyes had gone over the rounded grace of her figure, the delicate peach tan in her cheeks, the wide blue of her eyes. "I'd like to bet you've never even been to bed with a man." Ignoring her indignant gasp, he had gone on as he held the end of a fat cigar between equally chubby fingers, "But that's something that could be remedied. All you have to do is be nice to a few people I know, producers and other people high up in the entertainment industry, and you could just about write your own ticket to stardom."

"Thanks—but no thanks." Dani knew all too well about the "contacts" Emory Harden had in the entertainment industry. Some of the young models in his agency, mostly the ones from out of town, had gone that route and after a few months of contact with second-rate industry people had found themselves no nearer the motion-picture stardom they craved.

But Dani had no such craving. Her upbringing in

the movie capital had effectively killed any aspirations she might have cherished in that direction.

Sleep was tardy in coming as she tossed restlessly on the hard motel bed. If what Emory Harden had said was true, that her "innocent" image was no longer in style, how could she support her mother and herself, let alone pay for the treatments Marsha needed? She was trained for nothing except the holding of muscle-straining poses, the flashing of smiles that reflected none of her inner feelings.

She didn't remember, next morning, just when she had fallen into the deep and dreamless sleep that left her amazingly refreshed and almost optimistic as she set out after an indifferently served breakfast at the small motel's coffee shop.

"The coast road's a prettier drive," the service-station attendant told her while she waited for her tank to be filled. "Doesn't take much longer, either."

"Thanks. Maybe I'll take that route," Dani smiled as she paid him. She wanted to reach her destination as soon as possible, but she still needed to think about what might greet her once she got there.

Or maybe "who" should be substituted for "what," she reflected as she took the turnoff that would lead her along the wild, rough coastline. The letter informing her mother of Henry Benson's death had been signed by a Grant King, and bore the printed letterhead of Copper Canyon Ranch. Dani could still visualize the neatly typed words in her mind's eye.

Dear Mrs. Benson:

I very much regret having to tell you that Hank Benson died at his home here on February 19 of this year. His demise was too sudden to notify you before the event, and I have only recently discovered your address among his papers. Please be assured that all arrangements were made in accordance with his wishes, and that I personally feel the loss of a good friend.

Sincerely, Grant W. King

A good friend indeed, Dani almost snorted, her fingers gripping the wheel tighter. Grant W. King evidently didn't know that Henry Benson had kept her mother informed however sporadically, about his taking on of a raw young man who came job seeking into the canyon, eventually making him a junior partner in the ranch operation. It had been a lucky day for Grant W. King, she fumed, when he wandered onto Copper Canyon Ranch and worked his way into the old man's favor! Now he considered himself king of the castle. . . but he'd soon be toppled off that castle when Dani reached the ranch. She knew nothing about the law, especially in Canada, but there must be some kind of inheritance rights. She was determined to fight Grant W. King all the way, if necessary; not for her own sake, but for Marsha's. Just a small percentage of the prosperous ranch's income would, she was sure, be ample for her mother's treatments and would enable the invalid woman to live in reasonable comfort the rest of her life.

Resentment bubbled on the back burner of her mind as the miles passed under the wheels of the small but powerful sports car. She sidetracked Portland, Oregon, and skirted Seattle, Washington, in her drive north, stopping to rest and relax and call Marsha each evening. Her mother sounded anxious each time Dani spoke with her, but not on her own account. She was being well taken care of by her sister, Ada Parker, who had agreed to come from her Palm Springs home while Dani was away.

On the fourth night, still dizzy from the magnificence of the mountain scenery through which she had traveled, Dani made her last overnight stop at Kamloops, British Columbia's southerly cattle center. She stayed at an inexpensive motel not far from the road junction on which she would branch north on the following morning.

"Road's likely to be flooded around those parts," the laconic service-station attendant observed as he filled her tank next morning. With a bleak glimmer of amusement, Dani reflected that her sole direct communication during the past few days had been with motel keepers, indifferent waitresses, and attendants such as the one who now gave her a slow appraisal from the top of her blond hair, shining after its shampoo the previous night, to the tips of her Italian sandals peeping out from under the hyacinth blue of her well-cut pantsuit. The man's gaze made it abundantly clear that he liked what he saw.

"I've come too far now to turn back because of a little water," she said crisply, paying him and getting into the car. "We get floods in California, too, you know."

"Not like our spring runoff, though," he persisted with a lazy smile.

A vision of the snow she had seen yesterday, hanging ponderously from mountain crags, flashed across Dani's mind. But she switched on the ignition and said briskly, "I'll take my chances."

She hardly saw his shrug as she pulled out of the station driveway, and minutes later she was scoffing at his glum predictions as she swung north on the last lap of her journey. It was April and the sky was a deep prairie blue, the sun promising warmth as it rose. She should reach Copper Canyon in about five hours, by her calculation, allowing for slower travel on the stretch east from the main highway. She was well equipped for the probable absence of eating places along the way. The ham and cheese sandwiches she had persuaded the cook to make up at the café where she had eaten dinner the night before nestled alongside a full flask of coffee on the passenger seat beside her.

It was already afternoon when she reached the turnoff onto the subsidiary road that would lead her to the yet narrower final approach to the hamlet of Copper Canyon, which was a mere thread of black line on her map. So far the road had been good, but now she began to notice the swelling creeks that cascaded under the narrow bridges she crossed, the stretches of water lying with deceptive calm on the flatland beside the banks they had burst. Hunger forced her to park to one side of the road, and while she munched on the sandwiches she contemplated her situation.

If this traveled highway was showing increasing signs of the runoff the service-station attendant had mentioned, surely the side road would be in worse condition. Should she heed his advice and turn back? Her eyes swept the terrain surrounding the car. The beautiful mountain country was giving way to rolling hills and grasslands far ahead. Maybe the worst was over. She had come too far to be turned back so close to her goal, and her cash supply was far from sufficient to support a motel room in Kamloops until the flood season was over.

Leaving half of the coffee in the flask, Dani smudged a light coat of lipstick across the fullness of her lips and ran a comb through her shoulder-length hair before starting the car with a decisive switch of the ignition key. Come hell *or* high water, she would reach Copper Canyon within a couple of hours, or die in the attempt.

The latter fate seemed most likely, she decided ruefully an hour or so after turning reluctantly onto the graveled surface of what was little more than a track signposted Copper Canyon 25—whether the 25 related to miles or to the metric kilometers Canada had adopted, Dani wasn't quite sure, but either way the distance hadn't sounded too great. Now, as she struggled to hold the wheel steady on ankle-deep mud, she lost track of time and distance. So hard was she concentrating on following the barely visible track ahead that it was some time before she noticed the disappearance of the sun, and the lowering of clouds that presaged the large raindrops suddenly spattering on the windshield.

"Oh, no," she groaned, reaching for the wiper switch and glancing quickly at her watch before clutching the bucking wheel again.

Three-thirty! Yet the outside light had the quality of dusk before dropping into the darkness of night. The engine stalled and she gunned it rapidly to life again, sending the car forward in an uncontrollable spurt, wheels riding slickly through the mud cover.

She stared in helpless horror as the vehicle teetered momentarily on the edge of the deep ditch that had been her guideline for miles, then plunged wildly down its steep side and came to a jarring stop at its thickly mudded bottom, throwing Dani forward and sideways. The last sound she heard was the reverberating crack as her head hit the door support.

SHE WOKE to the muffled shout of a man's voice and the louder crunching of metal close by. Struggling to consciousness, Dani forced reluctant lids open on a scene that completely bewildered her.

She was in her car; that she knew because one hand was still tightly clenched on the familiar wheel. But why was the car tilted at that angle, and why did the phantom figure of a man guide the equally ghostlike form of a horse up and away from the car? Her head throbbed horrendously as she peered through the gloom, her brain sluggishly trying to decipher the messages her eyes were sending.

The grinding sound of tearing metal came again and she covered her ears with shaking hands.

"Don't—oh, please, don't," she moaned, wanting desperately to slide back into a state of not-knowing.

Then the noise stopped, and she opened her eyes again when a rough male voice said from the far side of the car, "Are you all right? Stay where you are— I'll come in and get you."

Dani couldn't have moved to save her life; which seemed to be precisely what the stranger was intent on doing as he put one knee on the passenger seat and stretched out long arms to ease her from under the wheel.

"Are you hurt anywhere apart from your head?" the voice came again.

Dani managed a whispered, "I—I don't think so."

His grunt could have meant anything, but in another minute her own raincoat, which she had stashed in the back seat, was being fastened around her throat.

"I'm going to lift you out now, so put your arm around my neck," the gruff tones said close to her ear, and obediently she lifted her left arm to twine it across the sodden shoulders of his rain cape. Where her fingers touched the warm skin of his neck, it was dry. Because of that wide-brimmed hat he wore, she decided hazily as she felt herself lifted lightly, weightlessly, and taken from the car.

Her breath drew in sharply when stinging rain bit into her upraised face and she instinctively turned her head into her rescuer's shoulder, gripping him more tightly as his feet slithered in the mud down which her car had rocketed. At the top of the rise the most enormous horse Dani had ever seen awaited them, a rope dangling from somewhere on the saddle.

"Can you hold on if I put you up on Josh?"

"Josh?" she questioned stupidly.

"The horse." There was a faint touch of impatience in his tone. "He won't hurt you."

"I'll—be all right."

She found herself hoisted unceremoniously onto the soaked saddle, and the instinctive shifting of the animal under her was brought to immediate stillness by a tersely worded command from his master. Moments later, the stranger lightly mounted the horse, settling intimately behind Dani. It was a situation that could be embarrassing, Dani thought light-headedly, but her rescuer's thoughts seemed far from her own as he spurred the horse into determined action.

"Where are you taking me?" She turned her head toward him, raising her voice against the constant hiss of falling rain.

"To a place nearby where you can dry off and shelter for a while." His breath created an area of warmth near her ear as he bent to talk to her. "Where were you headed?"

"Copper Canyon Ranch—is it near here? I lost track of mileage when I started to battle the mud."

"Are they expecting you there?" His body had seemed to stiffen behind her.

"No. No, I. . . ." Caution stilled the words on Dani's lips. It could be hazardous talking freely to a stranger on the streets of Los Angeles, let alone confiding to this man from nowhere that in the whole of this wild country not a soul knew or cared about her existence. "That is," she amended hastily, "no one knows exactly what time I'll be arriving. Only that it's today. I imagine they'll be starting to worry about now, wondering what's delayed me."

His disconcerting deep-chested chuckle tingled against her shoulders. "Anybody from around these parts knows that no one with half a brain in her head would contemplate driving the side roads north of Kamloops in the runoff season. Spring in California is quite a bit different from spring in the Chilcotin."

Dani's head jerked back and up. "How did you know I'm from California?"

She sensed his shrug under the rain cape. "Your license plate gave me that information."

"Oh." Dani subsided against the muscular figure behind her, the only way to go because the high western saddle, not made for two, chafed the fine skin of her thighs when she held herself away from him.

Maybe Marsha Benson, with her long-nourished fantasies of white-slave traders, had been right after all in dreading this solitary journey for her daughter. Thoughts of her mother brought weak tears to mingle with the steadily falling rain on Dani's cheeks. Not even the vast stretches of desert to which those legendary maidens had been carried off could compare with the utter and complete isolation of this landscape, with its secretive arching of pine branches leading to dark, unknown places. Places where bear, coyote and cougar might lie in wait for the unwary.

Unwary was exactly what Dani was where the vast

Canadian hinterland was concerned. Memory stirred as the stalwart Josh trod up rises fringed on either side by mournful, dripping fir trees—memories of spine-tingling movies seen years before with just such a background. How could anyone live in a place like this? Evidently the man behind her did; he seemed to know his way around the terrain that was completely obscure to her. What did he do for a living? What *could* he do for a living in this untamed land? Hunt? Fish?

"This is it," the gruff voice said from behind her ear, and her eyes strained forward in the waning light.

What she saw was far from reassuring. In a clearing to the left of the rough trail they followed squatted a small broken-down cabin, flanked by a lean-to shed that sagged dangerously at one corner.

"This is where you live?" Dani asked in an incredulous squeak, twisting her head around to stare round-eyed into his shadowed features under the broad-brimmed hat.

"Sorry it doesn't meet your high standards," he returned dryly, "but as the sailors say, any port in a storm. Stay there until I get a light going." So saying, her rescuer swung himself down from the horse, leaving her with a strangely bereft sensation as he strode purposefully to the cabin door and thrust it open.

Long minutes passed during which Josh, the horse, shifted restlessly under her as if scenting the dry hay awaiting him in the tumbledown shed and resenting the presence of her light body on his back, which kept him away from it.

Light sputtered in the small square window of the derelict cabin, but considerable time went by before the man's tall figure reappeared and crossed to where he had left Dani on the horse.

"You can go in now." He reached for her, hands firm and hard on her waist as she slithered down from Josh's back. "I'll light a fire as soon as I've seen to the horse."

Dani stumbled toward the welcoming light, her feet twisting on the root stumps of trees long gone, and stood blinking in the low doorway. The lamp the stranger had lighted hissed and spluttered on a square, plain wooden table in the center of the room. A black potbellied stove near the far wall was flanked by two high-backed wooden chairs, one an ancient rocker, the other equally aged but with straight legs. An old Welsh dresser stood lopsidedly against the wall immediately to her left, and her eyes went finally to the roughly made bunk bed in the corner nearest the stove.

How could any self-respecting man bear to live in a hovel like this? Still standing just inside the door, she shuddered. She didn't know what kind of man he was. He might be a fugitive from the law, for all she knew, hiding out in this desolate place where he could be sure no one would find him. Her thoughts spiraled hysterically. He could be a murderer, a thief . . . a rapist.

Dani swallowed convulsively and took a backward

step, barely stifling a scream when she came up against his hard unyielding figure.

"Don't touch me," she gasped, twisting away from the heavy touch of his hands on her upper arms and catapulting herself farther into the lamplit room.

He seemed more amused than offended as he came inside and closed the door. "I seem to recall that you didn't mind my touch when I was taking you out of your car and bringing you here."

Seen in the soft glow of the lamp, his cape-clad figure seemed more hugely menacing than ever. "I—I wasn't myself then," Dani gulped, her eyes showing the white of her fear as she glanced nervously around the small room. "I didn't know you were bringing me. . .here."

"What's wrong with. . .here?" he mimicked in his deep voice, turning away as his hand went to his hat to set it on one of the wooden pegs behind the door. Dani had a momentary glimpse of black hair—hair as black as night—before the cape was lifted from his shoulders and hung in the same place. She didn't quite know what she had expected. . .maybe a faded, well-worn work shirt torn in places, with pants to match. But the dark blue and white check of his shirt, stretched over muscular shoulders, seemed whole and comparatively new, if wrinkled from wearing and dampness. Matching lighter blue work pants molded to lean male hips spoke of some kind of care in selecting his wardrobe, but far from consoling Dani this thought made her heart beat faster in panic. Any man who lived in these conditions yet cared about his appearance must be on the run from the civilized world.

He turned back to face her and her eyes widened again in fright as they went rapidly over features half-obscured by several day's growth of black, stubbly beard, which did nothing to disguise the firm jut of masculine chin, the forthright straightness of his nose, the lift of broad forehead shortened only slightly by the reluctant curling of black hair over it.

Noticing her shiver, he went noisily across the bare wooden floor in his high-heeled leather boots. "I'll light the stove," he said in his husky man's voice, "and thaw you out a little."

Dani stared numbly after him. It was his eyes that had sent that final tremor through her. Dark to the point of blackness, they seemed to see through her, down to where every emotional instinct she had was telling her to be wary of this man.

Knees threatening to collapse under her, she found her way to one of the two armless wooden chairs pushed under the central table, scarcely hearing the protesting squeak of wood on wood as she pulled it out and sat, shaking, on its hard seat. Her eyes sought again the tall figure bent over the rusted black stove, and she knew with inevitable certainty that in any showdown of physical strength the stranger was ordained by nature to win. Even if she could escape from the close confines of the cabin, where could she go? She had lost all sense of direction, and the greater fear of the unknown wilderness out there weighed more in the balance than her apprehension about the man who now straightened with a satisfied grunt from the greedy crackle of dry wood in the stove's hungry maw. The black eyes swung around on her appraisingly, so that she was suddenly conscious of the lank strands of blond hair plastered around her face, the sodden state of her raincoat.

"You'd better take those wet things off," he said decisively, but Dani pulled the edges of her coat closer around her in an unconscious gesture of protection.

"No! I'm—all right."

He turned completely to face her, thumbs hooked confidently into the dark leather belt encircling his waist. "The last thing I need right now is a sick female on my hands. Either you take your wet clothes off, or I will."

"You wouldn't dare!" Dani whispered dryly, but her eyes went to the hard bulge of muscle on his upper arms.

"Would you like to try me?" he mocked, confident in his male superiority. "Well?"

Dani licked the suddenly dry surface of her lips. "I'll—take off my coat. I'm dry underneath."

To her surprise he accepted that gesture of compliance and turned to the primitively made row of cupboards above the sink situated beneath the small, square window that gave on to the front of the cabin. While Dani slid the sodden wetness of her raincoat from her shoulders, he rummaged in the cupboard's interior and brought out two ancient-looking cans.

"Corned beef and—" he scrutinized the faded label on the second can "—cut green beans. Okay?"

"What?" Dani blinked in bewilderment. "Oh, I

don't think you have to bother with a meal. If you'll just take me to Copper Canyon Ranch, I'm sure they'll—''

His harsh laugh interrupted her nervously controlled words. "You can forget about Copper Canyon Ranch," he told her with brutal frankness. "At least for a few days. The road's washed out between here and there, and they won't be sending any search parties out for you.''

"I told you, they're expecting me." Dani licked her lips nervously again, and the black eyes swooped and fastened on their soft fullness.

"I doubt it. People in this kind of country are apt to assume that even greenhorn visitors have more sense than to arrive when the spring runoff is at its height. Not even the dizziest of Grant King's girl friends would make that kind of effort. That's what makes me think you're...mistaken...in thinking he's expecting you. He'd have come down to Kamloops to meet someone as—'' the black eyes roved lazily across her face and tautly held figure ''—pretty as you.''

Dani's brain ticked over faster than it ever had in her life before. If she told him the truth—that she had come here, naturally uninvited, to claim the bigger portion of the ranch Grant King now controlled—she would be at his mercy. If, on the other hand, she—

"All right," she conceded, casting her eyes downward demurely. "Grant isn't actually expecting me at this time. I was supposed to come in a week or two, but we—well, when you're engaged to be married, you aren't very sensible about things like spring runoff. Maybe you know the feeling, Mr....? Are you married?''

His eyes had narrowed when she mentioned her engagement to Grant King, but it was to the last question he addressed himself. Lifting his gaze to glance around the primitive interior, he mocked, "Do you see a wife around anywhere?"

"I—I just thought you might have left her somewhere.''

"Like a package to be collected later? No." A wicked-looking knife carved precise slices from the block of corned meat he had turned out of the can. "If I had a wife, she would be here sharing my bed and board."

His emphasis was on the word "bed," and Dani had an involuntary vision of the man opposite her in intimate contact with the woman of his choice. That the choice would be his she had no doubt. The broad frame that exuded masculinity in all its aspects would make that an accomplished fact.

"You wouldn't exactly be providing a palace." She looked disdainfully around at the ancient and sparse furnishings, the bare wood floor, the rusty black stove that gave off a warming glow from the wood he had fed into it.

"Which is probably why no woman has seen fit to marry me," he returned without rancor. "It would take some kind of woman to fit in with my life-style." He placed two thick slices of the beef on a small plate and added half of the green beans, heated on the stove in a battered pot, then pushed the plate across the rough table. "This is the last can of meat, so eat your fill. Two nights from now, if we're lucky, we could be eating whatever I can catch in my traps or shoot with my rifle."

So he was a hunter, a trapper! Ignoring his proposed menu of wild game, Dani stared at him across the table. "Two nights from now I'll be eating dinner at Copper Canyon Ranch," she stated unequivocally, and was irritated by the sureness of his headshake.

"I'm afraid not. The way conditions are, it could be a week or more before you see Copper Canyon Ranch."

CHAPTER TWO

"I DON'T BELIEVE YOU," Dani said dazedly. "This place can't be that far from the ranch. I must have driven most of the way before I landed in that ditch."

"Half a mile can make a difference in this country," he told her in a laconic drawl, bending his head to the plate of food before him. "There are two bridges down between here and there, and it takes time in these parts to get repair crews on the job. So you might as well resign yourself to sharing my humble dwelling."

"No!" Dani's eyes went involuntarily to the single bunk in the far corner of the room. "I—I must get to the ranch. I'll find my own way there if you won't help me."

"Don't be stupid," he said with a sudden hardness that sent a shiver of fear down her spine. "You'd be lost within two minutes of leaving the cabin, as well as up to your ankles in mud."

Dani realized the truth of this as he rapidly disposed of the scanty meal, and she wondered abstractedly, as he paced back to the stove to lift off a dented metal coffeepot, how he supported his huge frame on such meager fare. In a battle of strength he would win hands down. Certainly against her light-weight figure.

Her eyes strayed again to the solitary bunk in the corner, and he interpreted her look with deadly accuracy as he came back to the table and placed two man-size mugs on it.

"If you're worried about your virtue," he said mockingly, "don't be. I never make advances to a woman until I'm pretty certain she welcomes them."

And that must be practically always, Dani thought involuntarily, her eyes half-afraid as they went over the powerful frame, the hard-muscled shoulders that the blue-checked shirt did nothing to conceal, the deep chest that tapered to neatly tailored hips, the well-set head with its black, curling hair. But could any woman care for his jaw with its overlay of dark bristles that gave him a wild, unkempt look?

"Don't you ever shave?" she asked impulsively, and saw a wicked gleam come into his dark eyes.

"Only when absolutely necessary," he returned, so suggestively that she knew immediately the occasions when he found it necessary to shave off the harsh stubble that could damage a woman's more sensitive skin.

"Then I guess you don't shave too often," she said, mustering crispness as she reached for the steaming mug of black coffee. "Women must be few and far between in these parts."

His firm mouth parted in a smile that revealed strong white teeth. At least he cared enough about his appearance to brush them regularly! "True," he conceded blandly, "but quality's more important than quantity in my reckoning."

Dani stared in fascination as he lifted his mug and took a deep swallow of the hot strong brew. Black hairs sprouted lightly on the back of his workmanlike hand, and it needed little imagination to guess that it grew even more luxuriantly over the rest of him. As if party to her thoughts, he reached up with his free hand and undid the two top buttons of his shirt, revealing a thick fuzz of darkness on his tanned upper chest.

"What do you do for a living?" she asked abruptly, defensively rude.

"A bit of this, a little of that," he shrugged.

"Are you a...a trapper?" Dani's movie remembrance stirred in her mind as she recalled numerous scenarios that always ended when the Mounties captured their man. Only in this case they hadn't done a very good job in netting the man who sat at his ease opposite her. With every moment that passed she was more convinced that he was a fugitive of some kind. Why else would he be hiding out in this deserted neck of the woods? His speaking voice was gruff, but educated in the kind of school that would be unknown here. His clothes were good, even if his appearance was unkempt.

She had almost forgotten her question when he answered it in a laconic drawl. "I hunt a little, and trap a little," he nodded. "Most of the time it's the only way a man can survive in a situation like this."

A situation like this! Naturally a man pursued by the authorities would keep away from the civilized

areas where he would normally buy the staples necessary to sustain life in the wilderness.

"Wh-what's your name? You haven't told me
yet."

"You can call me Burt."

"Just. . .Burt?"

"Names aren't important here." Emphasizing
this, he made no inquiry about her own name, and
she sent him a frosty glance across the table.

"In that case you can just call me Dani."

"Dani." His firm, dark red lips formed the name
lingeringly. "It's an unusual name for a woman."

"My father's name was Daniel," she explained
shortly.

"And you were to be Daniel the second?"

"What's wrong with that?" she flared in defensive
wrath. "Wouldn't you want your child to be named
for you?" As soon as she had said the words she
made a mental retraction. This man quite possibly
already had a child, a son he had named for himself.

"My name doesn't lend itself to female deriva-
tives," he said mildly, then fixed her with a harder
stare from his dark eyes. "Suppose you tell me your
real reason for coming here? I doubt if you've ever
met Grant King, let alone become engaged to marry
him."

At her startled, wide-eyed look he went on more
softly, "News travels fast in this kind of country,
even to my ears, and if someone as well-known as
Grant King were that close to marriage, even the
coyotes up in the hills would have heard about it. So
what's your reason for coming to Copper Canyon?"

Cold fright blocked Dani's thinking processes so that she just stared helplessly at the black eyes narrowed speculatively on her. If she told him the truth, that no one in this godforsaken place knew of her existence, let alone that she was in the area, he would feel free to do whatever he willed with her. On the other hand...she put up a trembling hand to the bruise on her temple that was making her head ache.

"Don't waste your time making up any more stories," he said with barely concealed impatience, showing no glimmer of concern for her unconscious gesture of fatigue or the paleness of her face despite the heat radiating from the glowing stove. "I'm something of an expert on the inability of women to tell the truth in its plain state, so save yourself the trouble."

The arrogant statement sent all thought of prevarication out of her mind. "All right," she snapped, "I'll tell you the real reason why I'm here. My grandfather owned Copper Canyon Ranch until he died in February—"

"He *what*?"

Dani surged on, pausing only momentarily to savor the slack-jawed surprise on her companion's face. "Henry Benson? You must have known him if you know Grant King."

He nodded slowly. "Sure I knew Hank Benson— he was a nice old man. He didn't judge people because of what they'd been or how they lived in the present. I knew him well."

Tension slackened in Dani's body and she sank against the chair back as Burt spoke. This man had known her grandfather, had liked him; it was unlikely Burt would do anything to hurt her. At the same time she was glad that Henry Benson had made a friend of this man who had openly admitted that there was something in his background that would be looked at in askance by less tolerant people than her grandfather.

"Copper Canyon Ranch belonged to my grandfather, and then this—this Grant King came along a few years ago and wormed his way in until grandfather made him a junior partner in the ranch not long ago. Grandfather died without making a will, and now Grant King has taken over the whole thing. I'm here to see that we get our rightful share of grandfather's estate."

"We?"

"My mother and I. She. . . ." Dani bit her lip. Telling this stranger that Copper Canyon Ranch had belonged mainly to her grandfather was one thing, but letting him know that Henry Benson had left his only son's family destitute was another. "We want what's due to us," she ended with a firm upward tilt of her rounded chin.

"I see." One capable-looking hand rasped against the bristly chin. "You came here to force Grant King to give up the bigger part of the ranch?"

"Something like that." Dani's bright blue eyes faced the dark glitter in his. "Why shouldn't we have what's rightfully ours?"

The faint trace of a smile edged Burt's red-lipped mouth. "You might have a little trouble proving that Hank owned the bigger part of the ranch. When he came here and settled, no one bothered too much about legal documentation.''

"Obviously Grant King did when he took over control of the ranch," Dani retorted sharply. "But he's about to find out that I'm not as gullible as my grandfather was."

Renewed anger sent color to her cheeks, a sparkle into her eyes, and it was moments later when she became aware of the man Burt's enigmatic expression.

He said nothing, however, and rose to his feet with a noisy scrape of the chair legs against wood floor. "It's getting late—time for bed. We'll talk more tomorrow."

Dani glanced automatically at her watch and saw that it registered a bare nine-thirty. Bedtime came early in the Chilcotin! Her apprehensive glance backward to the rough bunk brought a sardonic, "I've told you not to worry about your virtue, whatever state it's in." A lazy thumb indicated a door beside the Welsh dresser that Dani had presumed led to a bathroom. "I'll sleep in there for now."

"In the bathroom?" she queried with a lift of her blond eyebrows, penciled to a light brown line.

Devilment danced in his dark eyes as they went over the newly dried silkiness of her hair, the azure blue of her eyes, the rounded contours of her lips.

"I don't offer the conveniences of a modern hotel," he said with a white-toothed grin. "Bathroom facilities are situated in the great outdoors."

"Oh." Dani drew a deep breath. "I'll find them."

"I doubt it." His large-framed figure went on booted heels to the outside door and extracted her blue raincoat from the wooden peg. "I'll escort you," he said blandly, holding out the coat invitingly to her hesitant figure.

Knowing that she had no alternative, Dani submitted to the humiliation of being guided by his firm hand under her elbow to the primitive facilities located some distance from the cabin. He must have cat's eyes, she decided as she stumbled the last few steps on her own.

Emerging from the roughly constructed outhouse minutes later, she perversely rejected the guidance of his hand and stepped out confidently toward the cabin. Her own eyes seemed to have adjusted to the night darkness that closed in around them, but her ankle twisted annoyingly on a tree root just as she reached the pool of man-made light from the cabin's front window. She pitched sideways and forward, and a strong hand shot out to swing her back and around against a rock-steady body that made no effort to release her.

"I—I'm all right now," she gasped, aware suddenly of her body's unconscious response to the hard male lines pressed intimately to the soft contours of hers, realizing too late that her twisting motions brought her ever closer to his implacable stillness.

"Are you?"

Dani thought irrelevantly that it was as well the rain had stopped as cool fingers lifted her chin, then clasped with surprising gentleness just below it. She blinked at the hazily illumined face just above hers, knowing in the split second before his head bent that the stranger would kiss her. In the same rapid fashion her mind calculated the risk involved in allowing a man obviously starved for female companionship to make love, however mildly, to a girl completely in his power.

Those thoughts became academic when his firm lips touched hers and teased lightly at the slightly parted opening of her mouth. The cool night air warmed under the touch of those firm lips as their pressure increased and took all logical thought from her. It was as if she were a being made of pure sensation, soaking up the male scent of him, even glorying in the harsh brush of his unshaven chin against the smooth texture of her skin. She had a sensation of weightlessness in the steel-clad arms that lifted her almost off her feet to be crushed to the hard length of him while his lips sent shocking tremors of pure sensuality to every tingling part of her.

No male had ever made such an all-encompassing experience of a single kiss, at least not the ones Dani had known. Her fingers gouged helplessly at the smooth pack of his chest muscles in an effort to still the whirling vortex her unschooled emotions pushed her toward, but it was finally Burt who lifted his head and pushed her slightly from him. The thick huskiness in his voice made her take a long, painful breath.

"We'd better go inside before I forget all the rules of civilized behavior."

Rapidly recovering now that she was no longer in

physical contact with him, Dani snapped, "It seems to me you *have* forgotten them!"

"Because of a kiss?" His deep mocking laugh infuriated her. "Did nobody ever tell you that's just a preliminary to—better things?"

"I'm well aware of the facts of life, Mr.—whatever your name is," she retorted furiously, turning her back on him and treading with care her way back to the cabin door. "I just think that both of the parties concerned have a right to choose their—their—"

"Lover?" he suggested softly from just behind her. She heard the door click shut with frightening inevitability. "If I were a betting man I'd lay odds that by the time you leave here you'll be begging to make that choice."

Dani spun on her heel to face him, contempt curling her lips. "You're very sure of yourself, aren't you? I hate to disappoint your male arrogance, but I'll be leaving here as soon as daylight comes. After that, you can deal directly with Grant King."

"What makes you think he'll have a desire to help you?" Burt mocked, his dark eyes glittering with amusement. "If what you tell me is true, the last thing Grant King wants is a legitimate heir to turn up out of the blue. No—" he shook his head conclusively "—your best bet is to stick with me. I'll think of some way to fulfill your dreams of being a wealthy cattle-ranch owner."

Dani bridled at the sarcasm lacing his assured statement. "They're not dreams, but facts. Grant King owns only a small part of Copper Canyon

Ranch, and I mean to see that we get what's coming to us.''

''Oh, you'll get what's coming to you all right,'' he returned softly, meaningfully, and Dani turned abruptly away and went to the ancient rocker set beside the glowing red of the stove.

''I'll spend the night here,'' she declared shortly, shedding her coat before settling into the creaking depths of the chair, willing her head not to turn as his booted feet crossed the floor and came to a halt beside her.

''You'll use the bunk,'' Burt told her evenly, evidently expecting her acquiescence.

''No, I'll. . .rest here.''

''If you're worried that I'll be tempted to climb in with you, forget it,'' he said briefly, impatiently. ''There's another bunk in there—'' his head jerked to the door beside the Welsh dresser ''—and I'll use that.''

''Oh.'' In that case, Dani would be more than grateful for the stretch-out comfort of the bunk, however roughly made. Her headache had dissolved into a dull ache behind her eyes, seeming to sap the strength from her limbs. She needed sleep, if only to replenish the brain cells that at that moment seemed too tired to cope with the jumble of new impressions clamoring for attention in her mind. ''I—I need my. . .things from the car.'' Things like a nightdress, toothbrush and paste, cosmetics to clean her skin.

''You'll have to sleep either in the raw or in your clothes tonight,'' he said with harsh indifference, bending to stack more wood into the voracious stove, his broad, capable-looking hand then going to adjust a lever jutting from the smokestack. "I'd advise sleeping raw—the stove keeps the room pretty warm."

"I'll keep my clothes on," she said in a voice almost prim, and felt the release of an unknown tension when the tall stranger walked toward the door opening off the main room.

"Please yourself, I'll say good-night."

"Good night."

Her ears strained to hear him getting ready for bed, but there was no sound apart from a gusty sigh after the two distinct thuds that signified the removal of his boots.

Still she sat there, not stirring until the deep breath of sleep sounded through the thin partition. At least now she could wash the day's grime from her face and arms. It was only as she raised a hand automatically to turn on the sink taps that she realized none existed. What she had assumed to be a regular kitchen sink was no more than an enamel bowl set into a depression in the wooden counter top beneath the window.

It seemed the last straw in the series of mind-boggling events that had occurred since her departure from the relative civilization of Kamloops that morning, and Dani gave in to the tears that filled and brimmed over from her eyes. Why hadn't she listened to Marsha? The man called Burt was far from her mother's definition of a white-slave trader, but was her situation very far removed from that of the young innocents who had been wafted away to those legendary dens of iniquity? She was alone in a wilderness cabin with a man who by his own admission was a fugitive from justice. He *had* admitted that, hadn't he...?

Huddled under the blankets of the bunk moments later, she tried desperately to recall his admission of being an escaper from the law, but her lids refused the command of her brain and closed inexorably over the bright blue of her eyes.

To HER OWN SURPRISE, Dani slept soundly and without dreaming. Her nose twitched before her eyes opened, and she savored the aroma of freshly brewed coffee before being brought abruptly to jarring wakefulness by a man's deep-toned voice.

"Need some coffee to get your eyes open?"

Her eyes opened without the aid of the coffee he proffered. Memory rushed back as she took in the beige twill of his work pants, the matching light-colored shirt fitted tautly to shoulder muscles as he bent over the stove and removed the coffeepot. Greater shock widened her eyes when he turned and looked full at her. Under the black eyes that glinted even in the dim half-light filtering through the small window, his chin and jaws were clean-shaven. It was like looking at a stranger she had never before laid eyes on, and she lay speechlessly watching him as he approached noisily across the floor and held out the steaming mug.

"Here, maybe this will help you find your tongue. If you're always this quiet in the morning, you'll be a godsend to some man one of these days."

Conscious of the fact that her habitual neatness and caring for her clothes had prompted the removal of her outer wear before getting into the bunk the night before, Dani edged up on one elbow, holding the blankets close to her throat as she reached up with the other hand for the mug.

"Thank you," she said huskily, looking away from the mockery in his gaze, which went from the tightly held blankets to her blue suit and blouse draped neatly over one of the straight-backed chairs.

"So you decided to sleep in the raw after all?" he mocked, his eyes faintly speculative as they came back to her tumbled hair and rounded face that still held the softness of sleep. "But don't worry, I'm never in my best ravishing mood at this time of day."

Deciding it would be better to ignore his implication, Dani asked, "Wh-what time is it?"

"Time isn't important here," he shrugged, turning away to settle himself in front of his own coffee cup at the rough wood table.

"It is to me," Dani said hotly, revived after a deep sip from the mug. "I want to get to the ranch as soon as possible. I'm sure Mr. King will be very...grateful to you for caring for me overnight."

"Whether he would be or not isn't relevant to the situation." Burt swung around on the chair to regard her stonily. "As I told you last night, there's no way you can reach Copper Canyon Ranch until the bridges have been repaired. And that won't happen until the water subsides. Also, the road you got stuck on yesterday is a subsidiary one, the last one they make repairs to. So you might as well reconcile yourself to staying here for at least a week."

The blankets dropped slightly as Dani shot up to a sitting position, but she ignored them in her indignation. "I can't stay here—alone—with you! Even you must see that."

"Even me?" One black brow rose derisively.

"Look, you're not going to pretend you're a normal, everyday trapper, or hunter, or—whatever." She waved an impatient hand, then went on with slow emphasis, "I don't care what or who you are, or who you're hiding from. I just want to get to Copper Canyon Ranch."

"Oh, yes," he said softly, "to get your dues."

"What's wrong with that?" she asked, aggressively defensive. "Grant King owes me, and he's going to pay up or find himself in a lot of trouble."

Burt shook his head. "He's not the kind of man who takes kindly to trouble of that kind."

"Too bad," Dani retorted briefly, then looked at him curiously. "You obviously know Grant King—what's he really like?"

He grimaced and shrugged at the same time. "About usual for these parts. A man's man in a man's world. He doesn't go much for women."

"Probably because there aren't too many around here," Dani said dryly.

"That could be." Burt downed the last of his coffee and stood up, only slightly less menacing now than he had been the night before. "I don't know him too well."

Dani's eyes sought the dark glitter in his. "What does he think of you hi—being here?"

A sardonic smile edged the full-shaped red of his mouth. "He's been brought up in the kind of country where it's impolite to ask questions about a man's background. He accepts what I tell him."

"And that is?" she queried with a boldness she was far from feeling.

"That I need a little time on my own, away from the trials of civilization," he answered curtly, as if resenting her probing questions. "There's some warm water in the pan on the stove if you want to wash. I'll be seeing to Josh in the meantime, so you won't be disturbed. We'll see about breakfast when I get back."

Dani lay for several minutes after he had left, contemplating her spartan surroundings. His reference to the "trials" of civilization could be taken in more than one way. It wouldn't be hard to surmise that the rough and very tough-looking stranger who had rescued her from the morass into which her car had fallen had sought refuge from the law that would want to try him. In this primitive country, where men evidently lived without asking questions of their neighbors, he would be safe from the long arm of the law. Maybe he had posed as a writer, a poet who needed the solitude of these surroundings. For a fleeting moment she found comfort in the thought that Burt, whoever he really was, would hardly want to draw attention to himself by holding a female here against her will.

A cold chill descended on her immediately after the

thought flitted through her mind. No one knew that she existed, let alone that she was holed up in this desolate cabin miles from nowhere with a man who might have committed a dozen different crimes. A man who would be returning any minute from his chores with the horse.

The thought was enough to make her throw back the covers and step quickly across to where her clothes lay on the chair back. She had to get away from here, away from the man who cloaked himself in a mystery too involved for her to fathom. Her thoughts went on furiously as she pulled on the blue slacks and fastened her blouse to its topmost button.

His kiss the previous night had been warning enough. Even she, frightened as she was, had been helpless against the primitive response that had risen within her as his mouth moved with sensual surety on hers.

Her cheeks burned as she remembered her own initial response to his kiss, the way her body had arched against his in instinctive acceptance of his male strength.

She washed quickly in the bowl, finding an almost new cake of soap in the saucer, and used the faintly damp towel hanging from a wooden rack under the sink area. Burt must have used the same towel for his needs while she slept, but there was no other in view, so she toweled her face and arms dry with it. Before she had time to speculate again on his reasons for living so primitively, Burt thrust the door open and cast only a slightly mocking look at her fumbling fingers fastening the buttons on her frilled white blouse.

"You have a suitcase in your car?" At Dani's cool nod, he picked up her keys from the cluttered counter.

"Where did you get those?" She snapped out the question unthinkingly, and he gave her a sardonic sideways glance.

"In the ignition," he returned dryly. "Would you rather I'd left them there for somebody else to find and steal your stuff?"

A glimmer of speculation lighted Dani's eyes. If he had feared that somebody might come across the car, there must be some kind of traffic on the road. Surely any passersby would wonder where the driver had gone to and investigate the surrounding area?

"Don't get your hopes up. The only passersby on that road are vagrants, and their only concern would be that you might come back before they had time to sort out the stuff they could carry easily." He turned away from the swift disappointment reflected in Dani's eyes. "I'll get your things."

"And what am I supposed to do here while you're gone?" Her eyes swept scornfully around the tumble-down dwelling, snapping back to meet his when he gave a low chuckle.

"The place had needed a woman's touch for quite a while now. Why not clean it up a little?"

"I will not! You don't seem to understand who I am, and I certainly have no intention—"

"I understand who you are well enough," he said quietly, eyes narrowing. "But if you mean to take over the ranch and live in this country, you'll have to be able to take a little dirt when you're the only one available to clean it up.''

Ignoring the last part of his statement, Dani stared aghast at him. "What do you mean, stay here? The minute my business with Grant King is finished I'll be shaking the dust—*mud*," she amended, glancing through the clouded panes of glass at the lowering sky outside, "off my heels forever."

His eyes strayed to the delicately curved straps of her sandals. "Speaking of heels, I hope you brought some rubber boots with you. You'd lose those things after two steps in mud."

Distracted, Dani's gaze joined his and she knew with a sinking feeling that what he said was true. Even if she did make an attempt at escape she would become hopelessly mired in the thick gumbo outside. The rest of her footwear wasn't much better.

"I brought your purse in, by the way." Burt indicated the soft brown leather of her handbag propped against one of the bed supports.

"You've been back to the car already?" she frowned.

"No," he returned blandly, returning her stare. "I brought it with us last night, but forgot about it when I took care of Josh."

Forgot? Had he been truly forgetful, or had he left it out in the rickety horse shelter until he had time to examine its contents at his leisure? Again he seemed party to her thoughts.

"I didn't touch it apart from bringing it in," he said abruptly, turning back to the door before adding, "I won't be long."

Then he was gone, and Dani leaped into action. Rescuing her bag from the floor, she unzipped it and searched feverishly for her wallet. Her trembling fingers came up with nothing but the silk scarf she carried there for emergencies, her makeup bag and assorted notebooks and road maps. She sat down shakily on the unmade bunk and stared at the dusty floor.

So he was a thief, a petty one, besides being guilty of the bigger crime he must have committed to make him hide out in a place like this. Relief mingled with a strange feeling of disappointment. At least thieves didn't kill people...did they? Only if they're cornered, she recalled reading somewhere. But that was ridiculous, she chided herself, shaking her head in irritation; her instinct told her that he wasn't the kind of man to steal from houses, apartments. No, it would be something on a grand scale like salting away company profits for his own use. It wasn't hard to imagine him in a high position, a trusted position...now that he had shaved the frightening bristles off, she could picture him in dark-colored business suits, a dynamic executive.

She was still sitting there speculating when she heard him come back. A slow tremor that had nothing to do with fear started somewhere inside her. The feeling of disappointment grew to a tangible thing in her chest. Why did he have to be a thief?

"Will you open the door?" he called from outside it, and she got woodenly to her feet and crossed the room.

The soft blue leather of her suitcase was tucked

under one arm, the plaid travel blanket she had thrown into the back seat folded across the other.

Burt dropped the suitcase on the floor at the bottom of the bunk and tossed the blanket onto it. His eyes went then around the still untidy room and gleamed sarcastically when he turned them on Dani.

"You didn't even make fresh coffee?" His deep voice seemed to fill the small room, and she crossed her arms in front of her in a protective gesture that wasn't lost on him. "What's the matter? Cat got your tongue again?"

"The cat might as well have that, too," she snapped, stalking to the table and dropping into one of the side chairs.

"What's that supposed to mean?" he asked levelly after a slight pause.

"Don't pretend with me, Burt...whatever your name is. You must have known I'd find out about my wallet."

"Your wallet?" The bewilderment clouding his eyes might have looked genuine if she hadn't known better.

"Come off it," she said inelegantly, getting up to pace restlessly toward the stove, feeling its heat on her back as she faced him. "You just couldn't resist it, could you? Even though there wasn't much money in it, and you can't use the credit cards in this god-forsaken hole."

"Now just a minute!" In two strides he was in front of her, his jaw clamped to a hard line. "You say your wallet's missing from your purse?"

"You know it is!" She faced him with more confidence than she was feeling inside.

"If the wallet's missing, then it must have fallen out when you hit the ditch or while we were coming back here." His head swiveled back to the bunk, where her purse still lay. Grabbing her arm with bruising fingers, he pulled her across to it. "Was it zippered?"

"Yes, so—"

"Open it," he commanded harshly.

Not quite so sure of herself now, Dani pulled the zipper across with trembling fingers.

"Now take everything out and lay it on the bed."

With no thought of disobeying his grim order, she pulled out the scarf, the notebooks, the makeup bag, the—wallet. Her eyes widened as she stared down at the soft brown leather fold in her hand. How could that be? She would have sworn on a Bible that it hadn't been there on her first search. Swallowing, she looked up into Burt's stormy face, which was livid with anger.

"I—I'm sorry," she stammered. "It must have been—hidden between the notebooks and maps."

"Or were you just so anxious to prove that I was a thief?" The color had faded from his face now, leaving it with its basic weathered tan.

"I—"

"There's only one thing I'd ever want from you—" he jerked her head up with his fingers under her chin so that she stared right into his blazing eyes "—and that has nothing to do with money." His thumb ran roughly over her parted lips, making her gasp as sensation tingled along her nerve ends.

Before she had time to guess his intention, his hand slid across her cheek and curved around her nape, then his warm breath was fanning her mouth. "This should give you some idea of what I mean."

His mouth closed the inch-wide gap between them, and Dani was too numb to make even a token of resistance. It was as if she were watching a scene being enacted by two other people, a man's tall form bent to a woman's, his arms sliding down to encircle her smallness and pull her to the curve of his body.

It could have been seconds or long minutes later when Dani was brought to pulsing awareness of the real situation.

The harsh, punishing pressure of Burt's mouth eased abruptly when he sensed the submission in her suddenly pliant body, his lips softening as they moved provocatively back and forth over hers, his heart hammering against the palm she slid over his chest. Then her arms were around his neck, her fingers against the well-shaped outline of his head, pressing it down to the ready response in her lips.

When Burt would have rejected her invitation she pressed closer to his steel-covered thighs, feeling no sense of shame when he groaned and lifted his mouth to trail white-hot kisses across her cheek, his lips shaping the lobe of her ear. Time was nonexistent as they stood locked together in a closeness as primitive as the room surrounding them.

Dani blinked helplessly up at him when, with a raggedly drawn breath, he pulled her from him and unwound her arms from his neck.

"You really don't need much coaching, do you?" he said unsteadily, his eyes roaming over her flushed cheeks and wide blue eyes and glancing off the parted fullness of her mouth. "All innocence to look at, but I wouldn't lay bets on how little experience you've had with men."

"Maybe you should." Dani twisted away from him and stood looking down into the dull glow of the stove. "You might win a lot in a bet like that."

"I doubt it." Far from containing the humor she had expected, his voice was deadly serious.

Stung, Dani swung around furiously on him. "And what about you? How much money would I stand to win or lose in stakes like that?"

He shrugged and stepped past her to the cupboard above the window. "I'm no angel, either." He reached up and extracted a plastic package of rolled oats. "Porridge okay for you?"

"I'm not hungry," she said with a hint of the sulkiness he might have expected from the innocent he had thought her.

"Please yourself, but it's going to be a while till I get back with something for supper."

She turned her head quickly to look at him. "You mean...?" She swallowed nervously. "You're going to go out and *hunt* for food?"

"If we want to eat tonight," he returned dryly. "I don't know about girls from California, but I need reasonably regular sustenance. Now will you have some porridge?"

Dani held his gaze for a moment more, then her

eyes dropped. "I guess I'd better," she answered ungraciously, adding belatedly, "Thank you."

"Good. Maybe you'd like to make some coffee while I see to this."

He turned away before Dani had time to speak, and she looked worriedly from the battered coffeepot set at the back of the stove to his confident shoulders as he measured water into a pan from the bucket close to the stove. Was it possible her arms had lain on those shoulders just a few minutes before? That the man now placing the pan carefully on top of the stove to heat had tempted her more than any man ever had before?

CHAPTER THREE

Dani sat with her unfinished cup of coffee before her long after Burt had eaten his scanty breakfast and gone. This time he had left the voluminous rain cape on the peg behind the door, and emerged from his sleeping quarters at the side in a red plaid jacket such as she had seen in advertisements for rugged Canadian fishing holidays.

Her eyes went curiously to the closed door, the one she had foolishly mistaken for a bathroom door. His clothes must be stored in there, as well as the bed he had slept in last night.

Inquisitiveness got the better of her moral sense and she went to the door, the squeak of its hinges as she opened it stirring a recent hidden memory. She forgot that, though, when her eyes went around the cell-like space, falling on a rumpled sleeping bag on the bare wooden floor, an ancient dresser that took up most of the space along one wall, a crudely constructed clothes rack where man's clothing hung on wire hangers.

Dani shivered as she went farther into the small room. Evidently the partition dividing the cabin effectively blocked the stove heat from this area. Burt must normally sleep in the bunk he had given to her, and conscience smote her when she remembered the snug warmth of her own bed last night.

The clothes lining the rack were the average wear, she guessed, for a woodsman like Burt. Certainly the work pants in various colors and the shirts that hung beside them gave no clue to his real background. She laughed inwardly as she turned away. What had she expected? Fine wool suits with silk shirts and custom-made shoes? The footwear arranged under the rack was strictly serviceable for this country—ankle-length and calf-length boots make of durable leather to resist the destruction of snow, mud and dust.

Dani hesitated in front of the chipped wooden dresser. Hadn't she the right to discover as much as possible about the man who had brought her here? There might be papers in one of the drawers that had been carelessly closed as if Burt had searched hurriedly through them that morning. Having talked herself into it, she pulled open one drawer after another, discovering a jumbled assortment of men's socks and underwear, several wool sweaters in different colors, a couple of thick flannel shirts...but nothing remotely resembling a paper. In the long bottom drawer she stared in amazement at white cotton bed linen and a colorful red and black plaid bedspread. Why did Burt keep them tucked away in here instead of making his primitive way of life a little more comfortable? There was even a gingham tablecloth of large blue and white checks.

She was thoughtful as she went back into the bigger room. Of course! Laundering those items would pose a problem for a man intent on hiding himself away from the world. Everything on the clothes rack and in the drawers had been clean, but they were small items easily washed and dried in the cabin's main room.

Her eye fell on the Welsh dresser and the drawers under its flat top, which, like the sink counter, was cluttered with a hodgepodge of dust-covered articles. The drawers yielded more of the same: scissors, string, rubber bands, half-used candles, a few ball-point pens, but not one scrap of paper. The capacious cupboard underneath held an ancient set of chipped dishes of all sizes.

Sighing, she went back to the table and refilled her coffee cup with the dregs from the pot Burt had made. Whatever she found out about his past would have to come from him, and after that scene between them this morning, which had started with her mistrust of him, it was more than doubtful that he would confide his shady past to her.

When she remembered her response to the lovemaking he had begun in anger, a deep rose colored her skin. Not from shame...nothing that had come as naturally and powerfully to her could ever be a cause for shame. She had wanted him that morning more than she had ever wanted any man. In those minutes when she had pressed eagerly against his man's body, feeling his own response, it had been as if she was removed from all the inhibitions that had bound her before—her own natural aversion to casual sex, her mother's open trust that Dani would wait until a love as great as the one her parents had shared came along.

Maybe it was because of her sudden transition into the unbelievable world of this deserted cabin that she had given way to the wanton instinct she now knew lay deep inside her. A wantonness any of her previous dates would find hard to credit. But none of them had ever inspired. . . .

And neither would Burt again, she decided, swallowing the last of the coffee and rising to her feet with a quick movement. Her fastidious eye went around her dismal surroundings, noting the deeply ingrained dirt and thick covering of dust everywhere. If she had to stay here, and it seemed as if she must for the time being, she would make it as fit for human habitation as soap and water could make it.

Hours later, Burt had not returned and Dani seemed to have accumulated on her person all the dirt she had removed from the cabin. But there was satisfaction in her eyes as they went around the small abode, noting its transformed appearance. Late-afternoon light filtered more clearly through sparkling panes, the sink counter had been swept clean of the debris littering it, as had the Welsh dresser top, and the floor was as dust free as the straw broom propped beside the stove could make it.

But what mainly added to the cabin's hominess was the warm-looking bedspread falling over the edges of the crude bunk bed, obliterating the thick wooden posts supporting it. Under that and the blankets was the fresh crispness of white sheets and pillow. Dani had been too tired the night before to care much about the stale, slightly damp odor of the blankets. Tonight she would sleep between sheets that had the smell of the outdoors in them.

Tonight... how quickly she had become used to the idea of staying here with a man she had never heard of or laid eyes on before! Some strange sort of enchantment seemed to have enveloped her in its misty folds as she glanced around the room. The table had truly become a centerpiece with the blue-checked gingham cloth on which reposed a tall, thick drinking glass filled with fresh-sprouting sprays from a low-hanging tree not far from the cabin. Dani had also discovered, on her two journeys to the outside facilities, that the shed giving shelter to Josh also accommodated a goodly supply of root vegetables nestled in the straw closest to the cabin wall. Potatoes and carrots, cleaned and peeled, awaited Burt's arrival with the main part of the meal they would share.

She looked anxiously through the window before subsiding into one of the armless chairs by the table. Maybe he wouldn't even make it back before dark. Maybe Josh had stumbled and fallen and Burt was at that moment lying injured somewhere in the wilderness beyond the cabin. How impractical her hopes of escaping overland had been, she had realized on her trips outside. The clearing surrounding the cabin was relatively clear of mud, but just beyond that she had seen the deep-laid marks of Josh's hooves leading away from the cleared area.

She was studying the drastic effects of housework

on her neatly manicured hands when she heard the
sound of Burt's return. Jumping up, she leaped
across to the window and peered out into the gathering gloom. She caught a flash of Josh's hindquarters
as he was led into the humble shed that was his home,
then of Burt's tall figure a short time later striding
past the window.

Dani's breath tightened in her throat. It was
stupid, crazy, impossible that the sight of a man she
had known for less than a day could affect her this
way. Yet her eyes went hungrily to the broad set of
his shoulders under the plaid jacket, the strong male
shape of his legs tapering from under it. One of his
arms was outstretched, and she felt her stomach turn
in nausea as she recognized the small furred creature
dangling from his fingers.

It was the perfect Brer Rabbit, the subject of many
of her favorite childhood picture books. Pointed
ears, lying close to the thick brownish white fur,
topped black eyes that were obscenely open in death,
lips pulled back in the same agony.

Burt must have left the dead creature outside,
because he was emptyhanded when he pushed open
the door and came into the room. He took a couple
of steps before stopping incredulously, his eyes taking in, in a few short moments, the work it had taken
her hours to accomplish.

"Well, I'll be...." His dark flickering eyes turned
on Dani, noting with the same speedy precision her
change of clothes into form-fitting jeans and loose
pale blue top. "I've never seen this place look this
way," he complimented her, and something in his

eyes told Dani that he wasn't referring entirely to the scrubbed cleanliness of the cabin.

But the dead rabbit still filled her mind and she said coldly, "I had to pass the day somehow."

She turned her head away from him, but still felt his dark eyes burning against her skin.

"Where did you find all this stuff?" he asked quietly after a pause of complete silence.

"I didn't think you'd mind that I searched for them in your chest of drawers," she returned shortly, resuming her chair beside the table and looking up at him defiantly.

"As long as you found what you were looking for," he shrugged, his eyes holding a mocking light that said he knew she hadn't found what she was looking for—a clue to his past, his true identity. He strode across to the stove, which she had kept fed from the pile of wood stacked beside it, and lifted the lids on the two saucepans on the cool back area.

"I see you found the vegetable store, too," he remarked dryly, turning back to face her. "They should go well with what I brought home for dinner."

"If you're talking about the rabbit you murdered, you can forget it," Dani blazed whitely, clamping the full lines of her mouth tightly together as she stared down at the colored tablecloth.

"Murdered? Are you a vegetarian?" Burt's voice had grown tight, but she didn't care about that.

"No, I'm not a vegetarian, but—"

"I can assure you that the jackrabbit I brought back was killed as humanely as any steer in a slaughterhouse," he said tautly. "Anyway, it's the only meat we have, so—"

"Then I'll just eat vegetables," she interrupted crisply. "If you want meat you'll have to cook it yourself."

He turned curtly back to the stove and bent to rake through the glowing wood ashes with the metal poker she had used earlier. As he stacked fresh wood into the top opening, he said in a stiff voice, "That's no problem. But you're going to need protein before you leave here."

Strangely, she felt no great elation at the prospect of leaving the cabin as soon as the bridges were repaired. Since her cleaning episode the tumbledown abode had become hers in an odd kind of way, a way in which the man now striding to the door with grimly set face could never know. She had no way of knowing for sure, but her guess was that Burt hadn't lived here very long, certainly not long enough to accumulate the amount of dirt and grime evident in every corner of the cabin.

And that deduction immediately raised another question. Who had lived here before him? Had there been a woman's touch in the gleam of a polished stove, the smell of baking bread permeating the small structure, the sound of children's voices as they played around the cabin door? Perhaps the small room in which Burt now slept had been an addition to accommodate children. But where were they now, that mythical family of solid respectability?

She rose and went to the crackling stove, shifting

the vegetable pots farther forward on its cooking surface. She had no idea of how Burt would cook the rabbit he had caught, but the vegetables could be kept warm indefinitely once they were cooked.

Burt came in as she was laying knives and forks at either side of the table, and she looked away hurriedly from the pink white sections of meat he carried to the sink counter and deposited there while he crouched down before the cupboard and found a hefty frying pan. After giving her a hard-eyed look as he reentered the cabin, he seemed to make a point of ignoring her.

And that was fine with her, Dani fumed, rushing to raise the lids on the pots as steam forced them upward, colliding with Burt's burly figure as she turned away and met him reaching for the stove with his meat-laden pan.

Nothing in his expression revealed the slightest awareness of her as a woman as his arm circled her waist to steady her, but her nerve ends started up an excited jangle from the mere touch of his hard flesh against hers. She jumped away from him as if she had been stung, and caught a fleeting glance of mockery in his glittering dark eyes.

Finding sanctuary again at the table, she watched with smoldering eyes as he seasoned the meat in the pan after sliding it onto the hottest part of the stove. How could he stand there so impassively watching the little creature, which had been joyfully alive only hours before, seared to brown palatability? How could he stand the odor of its flesh as it browned in the cooking oil he had poured sparingly on it?

Sharp pangs of hunger contracted her stomach muscles as the smell of cooking meat drifted across to fill the cabin. She had had nothing to eat since the bowl of porridge that morning, and the cooking meat stimulated the appetite she had forced into quiescence all day. Really, the rabbit smelled not unlike the chicken she loved to eat.

But it wasn't chicken, she reminded herself sharply as Burt busied himself turning the delicately browned cuts of meat and seasoning them again. It was an innocent wild creature caught in the cruel trap of the predator man. Still her mouth watered.

"You don't have to eat it if you don't want to," Burt said laconically minutes later when he laid before her a steaming plate of crisply cooked vegetables and brown meat, its origin indistinguishable. He himself appeared to have none of her reservations, and he attacked his meal with all the gusto of a starving man.

And that's what he must be, Dani thought suddenly, having eaten as little as she herself had that day and with a much larger frame to fill.

Picking up her fork, she sectioned off a piece of potato and raised it to her lips, almost groaning aloud as the juices rushed to her mouth. It was only when the firmer texture of meat made her teeth chew more definitely that she realized her hand had lifted the knife and cut into the seasoned flesh without her volition. She waited for the nausea to rise in her throat, for her body's rejection of the food her mind found distasteful, but nothing happened. Conscious of Burt's regard, she sent a guilty glance across the table, expecting amused mockery in the dark eyes but finding instead a look that was almost compassionate.

"Don't feel badly about enjoying it," he said quietly, "even if it didn't come nicely wrapped from a supermarket shelf. It's a law of nature that small animals fall prey to the bigger ones in time of need."

"It wasn't nature who designed steel traps to catch the unwary," she snapped back at him, hating the weak tremor in her voice.

He shrugged. "Nature gave him the ability to invent ways of catching his daily sustenance." Now a faint gleam of mockery lighted the back of his eyes. "You would have starved to death back in our primitive days."

"It was different then," Dani argued persistently. "It was that or die."

"What do you think our position is right now?"

The sudden seriousness of his voice brought Dani's eyes up to meet the hard glint in his. She opened her mouth to speak, but no words came. His logic was too devastatingly true to argue with.

"Go ahead and eat," he said softly. "I can assure you the rabbit didn't suffer too much."

As if to set the example, he bent his dark head to his plate again, and for a moment or two she watched him. The clearly defined lashes covering his eyes were as thick and black as the rest of his hair; the bristles he had shaved off that morning were already sprouting again to give him that dark, wild look she had noticed the night before. Since taking off his jacket he had rolled up the sleeves of his drab-colored shirt over powerful forearms, and her pulse began an erratic rhythm that brought a flood of color to her cheeks. Had those arms really held her that morning, feeling like steel bands as they circled her eager body?

So engrossed was she in the sensual memories pounding at her brain that she was taken by surprise when he looked up suddenly, piercingly, into her eyes. There was no time to hide the soft wonder of the glow that filled her eyes, and there was a breathless silence of awareness as they stared at each other. Dani knew she should break that look, realizing with sudden clarity that the man opposite had the power to hurt her as she had never been hurt before. She had never responded so deeply and naturally to a man's lovemaking, and the thought frightened her. Shut off like this in a world apart from all she was used to, she was vulnerable to the assault he had made on her senses. But it was once again Burt who broke the mystical spell between them.

"Your food's going cold," he said quietly, yet giving the impression of abruptness, and she looked dazedly down at the meal she had barely begun to eat. Picking up her fork again, she made a tentative stab at the carrots.

"What do you do in California?" Burt asked in a conversational way, which she was sure he meant to reestablish her equilibrium. And strangely enough it did.

"I work for a modeling agency in Los Angeles."

Then she made a wry face. "I *used* to work for a modeling agency," she corrected.

"Oh? Why don't you work for them anymore?"

"Because I...." Her voice petered out as she remembered her reasons for leaving the agency. Did she really want this Burt to know that Emory Harden considered her too innocent-looking for today's modeling trends? Innocence added to her vulnerability as far as Burt was concerned, and she couldn't allow him that added advantage...always supposing he had that kind of design on her. "Something better came up," she tacked on coolly.

"Like a prosperous ranch in the Chilcotin?" he put dryly, then scraped back his chair noisily to rise and go to the stove where the coffee was already perking.

"Why not?" Dani rose automatically to get two mugs from the hooks beside the window. "My grandfather worked hard for years building it up."

"But you didn't," Burt said pointedly, turning from the stove and pouring the richly pungent brew into the mugs.

"So? Don't you believe in the laws of inheritance?"

He sat down again and drew the steaming coffee toward him before answering. "In certain cases, yes. I just think it's crazy for you to come from a modeling job in California and expect to run a ranch the size of Copper Canyon."

"I don't want to run it!" Dani cried in frustration, her blue eyes flashing sparks across the table. "I just want—"

"To live off the profits?" he cut in aggressively. "Do you think a man like Grant King will just let you walk off with the major part of what he's worked for all year?"

"He'd have his share," Dani insisted stubbornly. Then she looked at him suspiciously. "How come you're so anxious to stick up for Grant King's rights?"

Burt shrugged and took a deep swallow of coffee. "He's been pretty good to me since I came here." His head lifted and he looked almost lovingly around the cabin. "This place belongs to him, like most other things within a forty-mile radius."

"*Part* of it belongs to him," she corrected, her mouth pressing together in a tight line. "The larger part belongs to my mother—and to me."

"That's something you'll have to talk with him about when you see him." Burt dismissed the subject with a faint air of boredom.

"Wh-when will that be?" Dani stammered, astonished at her own lack of urgency about reaching the destination she had set out for. She wanted, inexplicably, to prolong this enchanted existence for as long as possible—though it was clearly a matter of extreme indifference to Burt, if his closed expression was anything to go by.

"As I told you, a few more days." He glanced around as if realizing for the first time that daylight had gone and that their table was lighted only by the glow from the open-fronted stove. "I'll light the lamp," he said heavily, getting up and bringing the old-fashioned lamp from the Welsh dresser where

Dani had placed it after buffing up its copper base. "You'd better watch in case I'm not here one night when it gets dark," he ordered without expectation of argument, and Dani pushed away the feeling of panic that threatened to swamp her and watched as he trimmed the wick and adjusted the controls until moments later the lamp spluttered into life, then settled to a flickering glow.

What would she do if Burt didn't come back one night? The small cabin was desolate enough in the daylight; at night it would hold all the childhood terrors of darkness. The thought sparked the memory that had been eluding her all day, and she asked suddenly, "Did you go outside during the night?"

His eyes swiveled from the lamp to her questioning face. "Why do you ask?"

"I... thought I heard someone moving around." More than that, her memory now distinctly reminded her of the squeak the door of his small room had made, the quiet but definite click of the outer cabin door closing. She had sunk back into sleep before the noise had penetrated her exhausted awareness.

"Nature doesn't always time her calls to coincide with our waking hours," he said with dry mockery, and Dani felt her face color to a deep pink.

"Oh, I... just thought someone else might have been... prowling around," she said lamely.

"We don't get prowlers in this area," he told her, emphasizing the cabin's remoteness. "There's never been a lock on the door."

"Really? I've never lived in a place where locks weren't needed." She knew that she was chattering inconsequentially, from nerves, but the silence that was sure to fall between them if she stopped talking was too frightening to contemplate at that moment. "Where my mother and I live in Los Angeles we have to keep triple locks on the outside door."

He gave her a keen, slightly surprised look before sitting down again at the table. "You live with your mother?"

"Of course. She needs me to—" she broke off and went to resume her place opposite him "—keep her company since dad died. She was very...dependent on him."

"That must be hard on your love life."

"My...?" She stared blankly at him until understanding dawned, then filled in crisply, "I manage."

"I'm sure you do." His eyes, shadowed underneath from the lamplight to one side of the table, went in mocking appraisal over her flushed cheeks and full-lipped mouth and down to the loose pale blue top that did nothing to obscure the soft curves of her breasts. "You must have very understanding boyfriends."

"I have a very understanding mother."

His mouth seemed to tighten to a hard line. "She feels the same way as you do about taking over the ranch?"

"Why shouldn't she?" Dani prevaricated, loath somehow to let him know that this was one matter on which the gentle Marsha would never agree to press. She had scarcely known her husband's father, and therefore felt she had no right to his wordly goods after his death. Not even to alleviate the suffering she endured every day of her life.

Dani lowered her eyes to the blue-checked cloth when her eyes stung with ready tears. "The money is hers—ours." She ran a shaky hand over her forehead. "She'll be worried about not hearing from me. If she calls Grant King and he tells her I haven't turned up...."

"Is she likely to do that, call him?"

Dani shook her head. "Maybe not for a day or two. I told her when I called her from Kamloops that I'd be in touch as soon as—as—"

"As soon as you've persuaded Grant to hand over the ranch to you?" his deep voice grated. "From the little I know about him, that could take some time. What do you plan to do if he refuses?"

"How can he refuse?" She raised her voice to a higher pitch. "He knows as well as I do that Copper Canyon Ranch belonged to my grandfather. There must be a law that protects us against a self-seeker like Grant King."

"There probably is," he said, a shrug in his deep voice, "but that kind of legal hassle could be costly if you lose. But—" a hard light came into his eyes "—maybe money is no object to you. I imagine models earn more than enough to keep them in... comfort."

His snide tone wasn't lost on Dani, but she held her temper and said coldly, "I believe top models do, as does anybody else at the top of his tree, but—"

"Are you trying to tell me you're not a top model?" he baited, black eyes gleaming. "The clothes you were wearing yesterday weren't bought in any bargain basement, and the car you're driving isn't your run-of-the-mill jalopy.''

Dani drew in a breath of irritation, regretting that she had confided so openly in this man who was virtually a stranger to her. ''In my profession good clothes are important, and the car was a gift from—''

''Your practice of another kind of profession?'' he suggested softly, eyes narrowing as they took in her quick flush of anger.

''How dare you!'' Dani almost upset the chair as she got wildly to her feet. Under her fury was the knowledge that there was some justification for Burt's assessment of her character, after the scene that had taken place between them that morning, and that flicked her temper to greater heights. ''Who are you to judge anybody else, even if what you're implying is true? Your own past obviously isn't something you're proud of, or you wouldn't be hiding out here in the back of beyond.'' When his head lifted in what she thought was denial, she went recklessly on, ''Why don't you tell me what *your* real profession is? Are you a rich man, poor man, beggarman or thief?'' Her emphasis was on the last category and she watched, nostrils flaring, for his reaction.

If her expectation had been that he would confess to one of the crimes she had accused him of, she was disappointed. But his next words proved that at least she hadn't been wrong in some of her conjectures.

He rose, too, and stood facing her, his back to the stove's heat. ''I practiced law in Boston before I came here, so that eliminates most of those categories."

"Except the last one," Dani shot back, too incensed at that moment to analyze her feeling of letdown in knowing that her original suspicion had been true. "What did you do? Embezzle a client's funds?"

A twitch along one of his closely clamped jaws was the only indication that her barb had hit home. "I doubt if a California-model-type girl would have the capacity to understand the motives that brought me here," he clipped.

"You're right," Dani scorned. "What good does all the money in the world do if you have to live like a hermit way out here? Knowing that you can never go back to the life you knew, the people who cared about you." She lifted her chin challengingly. "Or don't you have any family who might care about you?"

"I have a family," he bit off tightly, bringing his hands up to loop the thumbs through his tooled-leather belt. "I think they understand why I wanted to come here."

"Did you give them a choice?" she mocked. "Some parents can't see any wrong in their children no matter what they do."

"Then I guess I was blessed with parents like that." His deep voice held a tone of finality, and Dani dropped into the chair she had recently vacated. "What do you normally do at night around here?"

His brows rose in recognition of her change of subject, but the hard line of his dark jaw relaxed as he came to sit opposite her again.

"I read a little," he drawled laconically, and Dani's mind went to the stack of paperback mysteries she had examined cursorily before replacing them on the jutting upper shelf of the Welsh dresser. At the time she had wondered at his choice of literature, but of course if he was a lawyer.... That thought she put aside until she had time to think about it at her leisure.

"Nothing that we can do together?" she asked in all innocence, only realizing the implications of what she had said when her eyes met the meaningful spark in his.

"I mean," she added hastily, "cards, dominoes, that kind of thing."

"Maybe you'd know more about that than I would," Burt said, softly sarcastic as his eyes flicked over the crisp gingham tablecloth, the colorful splash of the bedspread. The implication was clear that Dani had gone beyond the bounds of good housekeeping to forage among his possessions.

"I happened to see a pack of cards and a cribbage board in the dresser drawers when I was cleaning up," she said with defensive loftiness.

"You play crib?" he asked, brows raised disbelievingly.

"My mother and I play all the time."

"In between your. . . other commitments?"

Dani glared balefully across at him, feeling a strong urge to lift her hand and wipe the knowing look off his face. Instead she drew a steadying breath

and asked, "Do you want to play or not? I just
thought it might help pass the time, but if you'd
rather—"

"We'll play," he conceded abruptly, and pushed
back his chair, tight-fitting trousers stretching tautly
over his firm-muscled thighs. "I'll see to the stove
while you get the board and cards."

Dani's eyes seemed drawn to the male symmetry of
his body as he bent over the voracious stove, stack-
ing wood into its capacious interior. She noted
with quickening pulses his smoothly muscular
shoulders that moved rhythmically with each bend
to the dwindling stack of wood, the flatness of
his hips encased in the firm twill of his work trousers.
Why did he have to be a refugee from all the mores
that civilization held dear? Even more shattering
to her was the wave of empathy that washed over her
with the remembrance of his lovemaking that morning. Despite his hermitlike existence, he was the
most exciting man she had ever met. The casual dates
she had known in California faded into insigni-
ficance compared with Burt. Two or three of them
had accused her of coldness when their swift rise to
passion had made her draw back. There had been no
holding back when Burt made love to her, making
the responses she had suppressed spring to vibrant
life.

She became aware suddenly of his questioning
look in her direction, the poised stillness of his body
as he seemed to delve into the privacy of the thoughts
reflected in the misty blue of her eyes.

"I...I'll get the cards," she said hastily, scraping

back her chair and going with jerky steps to the rickety dresser, rummaging there until she found the well-used cribbage board and faded pack of cards.

They might have been any isolated couple playing a card game by the light of a softly hissing kerosene lamp, except for the awareness that was like a tangible thing between them as they played the cards and toted up the score. The male shape of Burt's hand was more fascinating to Dani than his triumphant, "Fifteen two—fifteen four—fifteen six—and six for queens, which totals twelve and makes me a winner."

"This time," Dani conceded wryly, vindicating herself by being two games up.

Burt said finally, "I think it's time we called it a day." Although Dani knew it wasn't possible for human eyes to change color, Burt's at that moment seemed to darken in the light of the fitful kerosene lamp.

"Yes, I—I guess so," she said faintly, the smile fading from the wide blue of her eyes as he took two lazy steps around the table and bent to help her to her feet. Her heart did a crazy leap in her breast when his hands, instead of lifting, slid slowly up the bare contours of her arms. Her breath was like a wild thing in her throat from the feel of his dry warm fingertips against her skin, and a tremor ran through her as her eyes lifted to meet the wakening sensuality in his.

What was happening to her? How could she, always so self-controlled emotionally, suddenly let herself be affected so much by the presence of a man she hadn't known existed until the day before? She wanted to close her eyes to the nearness of him, but instead they dropped to the firm wide outline of his lips and she knew she wanted him to kiss her again as he had earlier in the day. And if he did, she would be lost. Lost in a world of sensation she had only guessed at before now. She ran a moistening tongue over her lips and gave him a quick upward glance.

"I—"

"Good night, Dani," he said huskily, and did touch his mouth to hers briefly before straightening and dropping his hands from her arms. The disappointment was like a blow to her midriff. "I'll get the flashlight," he added more clearly as he turned away.

Dani wished with a sudden flare of hatred that she could tell him she didn't need his company for the outside trek, but common sense told her that the walk, so easily accomplished in the daylight, would hold unlimited terrors without his stalwart presence.

Their mission was accomplished in silence, and they parted with another brief good-night before Burt disappeared into his small room. Dani gave a despairing glance at the dishes and pans piled on the sink counter, and decided to warm some water next morning to wash them and the dishes they would use for breakfast. A wry smile touched her mouth as she took a flimsy nightdress from her suitcase and threw it on the bunk. How quickly she had become used to doing without all the amenities of civilization she had taken for granted until now. Maybe something of her grandfather's pioneering spirit had filtered down to her!

That premise was severely tried minutes later when she decided frustratedly to wash herself in cold water. Although the chill had been taken from it because of its proximity to the stove, she still gasped as she splashed it over her face. The exercise had the effect of awakening her to tingling awareness, so she extracted her hairbrush from the suitcase and sat on the edge of the bunk to pull it through the dulled sheen of her hair.

What did a person do for baths around here, she wondered as her hand moved in an automatic, soothing motion. Burt certainly didn't give the impression of being a member of the world's unwashed—even his hair had felt clean and fresh under her fingers. The memory evoked by that thought was quickly pushed away. He had made it amply clear that he regretted that slip.

Maybe there was a shower enclosure outside, connected somehow to the stove's heat. She would have to check on one of her outside forays the next day.

More in the mood for sleep now, Dani blew out the table lamp and groped her way back to the bunk in total darkness. Burt was a quiet sleeper, she reflected staring into the blackness. After the initial noises of boots being removed and the rattle of hangers as he hung up his clothes, there was complete silence.

Or was he lying there awake, wondering how soon he could safely get rid of his unwelcome visitor? Her cheeks burned when she recalled her own eagerness to sample again his brand of lovemaking, an eagerness he obviously hadn't been keen to share. Yet for a moment she had been sure that his desire was as needful as hers.

Lethargy crept into her limbs, snug between the crisp cotton sheets, and she thought sleepily that she should be thankful Burt hadn't taken advantage of her obvious vulnerability. Most of the men she was acquainted with wouldn't have thought twice about taking gladly what she had so freely offered.

Why hadn't Burt, she wondered contrarily. Had he left a woman behind in Boston, a woman so important to him that no temptation, however strong, could lure him from her?

What a lucky woman, was Dani's last thought.

CHAPTER FOUR

WAKING TO UNACCUSTOMED BRIGHTNESS, Dani pushed aside her blond hair and blinked into the shaft of sunlight that slanted in through the small cabin window. It must be late, she thought, for the sun to have risen far enough to top the trees surrounding the clearing. She sat bolt upright on the hard mattress and listened for sounds of movement from the adjoining room, but there was only the sound of the wood hissing and crackling in the stove to break the silence of the cabin.

Realizing suddenly that she had no good reason to rise early in her mud-surrounded exile, she subsided on the pillow again and lay watching the ceiling thoughtfully, one arm behind her head.

Had she dreamed it, or had her sleep been interrupted earlier, as dawn filtered through the uncurtained window, by her own fearful mutterings? And had the big man's figure straightened from the stove and come to soothe her back to sleep?

"It's all right, Dani," the deep voice said in her hazy memory, "it's only me. Go back to sleep."

More real in her recollection was the light touch of his hand on her hair, the gentle strokes of warm fingertips against her cheek. She put up a hand now to where she fancied she still felt that gentle touch. For a man of his size, Burt had the ability to be incredibly tender.

The misty blue of her eyes went around the cabin's interior as she pondered the implications of the quickened beat of her heart, her pulse's increased rate when the firm-jawed face of her rescuer filled her mind. In no way could it be possible for someone like her, used to fending off the attentions of males who were considered sexually desirable by most of her friends, to have fallen in love with a—

Her eyes fell on a white piece of notepaper propped against the container of greenery she had placed on the table the day before. Throwing back the covers, she hopped barefoot across the floor and snatched up the scrap of paper.

"Dani, I should be back before dark. Help yourself to whatever food you can find. Burt."

Not exactly a love note, she decided ruefully before chiding herself for unrealistic expectations. A man bent on trapping food for his daily survival would hardly feel it necessary to couch a note to his unwelcome visitor in flowery terms. And he had made it obvious that her presence was unwelcome in his enforced solitary existence. Besides, there was the woman Dani was more sure than ever existed in his background, the woman who was probably waiting right now for—what? For his return from fugitive status? Or to join him in his exile?

No. Her eyes explored the small room, made only slightly more livable by her own efforts. The kind of woman Burt would love wasn't the kind who would live in these conditions. She would be elegant, sophisticated, sure of her place in society.

But why should she worry about the kind of woman Burt would prefer? Her thoughts took on a black aspect as she dipped water for washing into a pan from the bucket on the floor. Like a lot of the people she had met, Burt looked on models as females without morals or perception. He had made that only too clear last night when he suggested that her car had been a gift from a man in return for sexual favors.

Her blood boiled faster than the water warmed on the stove top, cooling only slightly when she discovered the half-filled percolator perched to keep warm at the side. The coffee tasted bitter from standing, but at least its zest helped to bring her to full wakefulness.

She glanced speculatively around the room. How could she fill in the long hours till he came back, probably with another revolting offering from his traps? The cabin was as clean and tidy as it was possible to make it without burning it down and starting again from scratch. Cleaning out and scrubbing the cupboards and shelves would fill an hour or two, but the rest of the day yawned emptily ahead.

Irritation welled up in her again. How dared he bring her to this off-the-map broken-down shanty and leave her here alone for all the daylight hours? Did trap lines have to be inspected daily? For the sake of the animals caught in them she hoped so, but Burt could hardly feel his time was well spent when his only prize yesterday had been a solitary rabbit.

Maybe he had a place farther along the trap lines where he took the fur-bearing animals he caught—lynx, beaver, mink or whatever was plentiful in the area. But where did he sell the skins? His only mode of transport appeared to be the horse, Josh.

Giving up on the questions that riddled her mind, she poured a generous amount of water into the sink bowl and, sure that she would have complete privacy, stripped and had a complete wash, which was the next best thing to a shower or bath. She tried not to think of the long, leisurely baths she had luxuriated in at home.

As she dried herself piecemeal on the towel shared with Burt, she frowned, reminded of Marsha and how concerned she would be when Dani failed to phone her yet another day. Would she get in touch with Grant King?

Her hand paused in midmotion, shocked into stillness by the realization that the crusade against the usurper of her grandfather's property no longer filled her mind exclusively. Almost every waking thought was connected with Burt, the man who had played on every emotional key in her repertoire. In a matter of days, hours even, she could be gone from this place, gone from Burt and his primitive way of life, gone from the most exciting man she had ever met.

"You're an idiot, Dani Benson," she scorned aloud as she dressed quickly in fresh underwear and the same jeans and top she had worn the day before. Even if he hadn't been committed to the woman in Boston, who was now a solid entity in Dani's mind, what future could there be for her with a man who had to spend the future as a recluse from the world as she knew it? It was fine and dandy to play at keeping house for a day or two, even considering the drawbacks of Stone Age facilities and loneliness, but that kind of existence would pall in short order if it became a steady diet.

Realizing with a self-mocking grin that she was erecting paper dragons, Dani set herself to the more mundane reality of filling her empty stomach with a large helping of the porridge she had disliked yesterday, but which she hated this morning with a passion. Her mouth watered at the thought of crisp bacon wafting its appetizing odor through the room, and eggs prepared any style, scrambled, fried, poached, made into fluffy omelets. And bread... thick-cut slices of the newly baked loaves her mother had made before her illness and that Dani herself still turned out when time permitted.

So vivid were her imaginings that the porridge went down as if it really were bacon and eggs and fresh-baked bread, but Dani sighed as she stacked her plate with the other dishes in the bowl she had emptied outside and scoured with cleanser she had found under the sink. Imagination could go only so far.

Leaving the dishes to soak, she made her first trip of the day to the outhouse perched among the trees, blinking in delight at the bright freshness of the day. Birds twittered and sang in the trees not far from the cabin as if they had found a new reason to live in the sun that sent its brilliant rays through the trees and dappled the rough ground with shadowed light.

The sky above was an intense shade of cloudless blue, and the ground under her feet no longer squelched as she walked. Soon she would be able to leave, to complete the mission she had set out on so many miles away in California. And that was what she wanted, she reminded herself firmly.

Cleaning out and scrubbing the shelves of the Welsh dresser occupied most of the morning, and she sat back on her heels before it at last and wistfully wished that she could complete the job with fresh shelf lining. But the small blue check of the original oilcloth had taken kindly to its wash. The dishes, too, took on new life from their belated introduction to soap and water, and Dani was well pleased with the results of her morning's labor.

The empty state of her stomach sent her foraging, just after noon, in the cupboard above the sink from which Burt had taken the can of meat and green beans on her arrival night. After setting aside the assorted cans of vegetables, her fingers encountered at the back of the shelf a small round tin. Her hungry eyes focused on and deciphered the tiny writing to learn that the contents were salmon pâté, "delicious as a spread on bread or crackers."

Ignoring the lack of the latter items, Dani feverishly opened the tin with the small key provided and dipped a finger into the brownish pink pâté. Its savory flavor was like manna on her tongue, and before she realized it half the can was gone.

"Oh, Burt, I'm sorry," she whispered guiltily, knowing that the can, however small, might have provided sustenance for him at some future time when he hadn't been able to catch or trap his daily food supply.

Disregarding the even more insistent clamor of her stomach, incited to expect a reasonable meal, she pressed the lid back onto the can and set to in a frenzy of guilt to clean out the store cupboard, too.

Ten minutes later she was staring in amazement at the contents of a metal canister from which she had pried the lid. Inside lay an unopened sack of flour and, glory of glories, several foil-wrapped packages of granulated yeast. Why hadn't Burt mentioned that he had all the makings of bread?

Probably because he imagined a model-type girl wouldn't know which side of the bread pan was up, she snorted indignantly. What wouldn't she give to present him with a crisp-crusted fresh-made loaf when he came home tonight! The thought no sooner entered her mind than she went into action, rummaging among the assorted pots and pans in the bottom of the cupboard and coming up with a battered round-shaped pan with the necessary high sides.

A strange sense of happiness descended on her as she busied herself with the ingredients for her bread making, and she caught herself humming a line or two from a popular western song she liked.

"So? How much more western can you get than this?" she mocked aloud as she began the mixing process.

Later, the dough placed close to the stove to rise, Dani wiped the perspiration from her brow and looked longingly at the sun-filled clearing in front of the cabin. What could be nicer at that moment than a relaxing fifteen minutes in the sun with a freshly brewed cup of coffee?

A hard-backed chair, she reflected fifteen minutes later, wasn't quite the same as a lounger in the sun, but at least she was out of the kitchen heat and feeling the surprisingly strong rays on her upraised face. Her eyes closed, and she wondered if the pioneer women in this area had ever done as she was doing now—relaxed temporarily from the never ending chores of caring for husband and children.

What must it have been like then, living and loving in an environment like this that could be harsh as well as beautiful? They were hardier women in those days, she thought sleepily. They had to be to survive conditions like these and bring up a family to boot. Her mind was filled with the picture of half a dozen brown-legged children playing in the sun, waiting with their mothers for the father's return from the day's labors. A smile curved her lips when she saw the young offshoots of their father run to meet him as he came home swinging an ax, grinning when the fair-haired daughter he swung up into his arms squealed as he rubbed his black growth of beard on her delicate skin. . . .

Dani opened her eyes with a start, blinking dazedly around the small clearing circled with trees and undergrowth. She must be going crazy; she could have sworn she heard the high-pitched squeal of the little girl's voice as her father hugged her.

It happened again, and Dani looked fearfully across the clearing to her right, her heart jumping when her eyes focused on the figure of an animal standing staring at her from under the inner circle of trees. Terror froze her to the seat of the chair as her eyes flicked nervously over the statuelike animal. Did coyotes have a shaggy coat of black and white— mutely appealing eyes of tender brown—a tail that wagged tentatively when a strange human rose from a high-backed chair and retreated toward the safety of the cabin?

Dani licked her dry lips and wondered whether the creature would dive in line with her throat if she moved any faster than the snail's pace her leaden feet carried her in the direction of safety. She slid out a groping hand and felt for the door latch, breathing easier when her fingers brushed its rusted iron.

"Steady, boy," she said in a voice far from steady, and lifted the latch preparatory to sliding into the cabin and slamming the door shut.

She froze again when an ingratiating whine came from the black and white body, and it was then that she realized only three paws were planted firmly on the grassy undergrowth. The other was held up with an unconscious appeal that immediately melted her fear and sent her stumbling across the uneven ground toward the animal. He made no aggressive move- ment, instead standing quietly until she came up to him, then wagging a shaggy tail as he bent his ears back and whined softly deep in his throat.

"What's the matter, fella?" Dani knelt in front of him, ignoring the damp patches of dirt that would adhere to her jeans, running a tentative hand across his rough head while talking soothing nothings.

"Wasn't I stupid? I thought you were a coyote, when all the time you're a beautiful sheep dog."

Where had he come from? He appeared well fed, if muddy in places, so he must belong to somebody. But to whom? She would have seen him before if he were Burt's.

The dog lifted what was evidently an injured paw farther, unbending the lower half, which had been tucked away out of sight.

Dani moaned in horror when her eyes fell on the ragged, gaping wound gouged into the paw, nausea rising forcefully to her throat. That the animal expected her to do something about it was obvious from the pleading look in the brown eyes, the encouraging whimpers from the throat. But what?

"I'll get some warm water and bathe it for you, boy," she promised softly, but found as she walked away that the dog limped along close by her heels.

He followed her into the cabin and made a halting tour of its confines, wagging his tail like a plume as he sniffed at the closed door of Burt's room before making a cursory inspection of Dani's suitcase, bed and the covered dough bowl by the stove. Then he looked up expectantly.

"All right, I'll see what I can do for you, fella." Setting a pan of water to heat on the stove, she searched through the cupboards for some kind of first-aid kit, but it seemed that Burt scorned the possibility of emergencies arising. As a last resort she took one of the frayed but clean tea towels from a drawer under the sink and tore it into strips without compunction. Using the widest strip as a wet cloth, she knelt and gently bathed the wound, although the dog himself had already used his tongue to good effect.

He waited patiently while Dani tied strips of the towel tightly around his paw and licked her hand when she said finally, "That's the best I can do for you, boy. Maybe Burt can think of something better when he comes home."

From his traps, she added sourly to herself as she twitched one of the dark-colored blankets from the bunk and folded it to make a bed for the dog beside the stove. He settled happily on it, the bandaged paw stretched out before him. Then Dani froze halfway to straightening up, her eyes seeking again the bandaged limb. At the back of her mind she had been assuming that the dog had been involved with another animal, wild or domestic, in one of the fights that seemed to come naturally to them.

But wasn't it just as possible that one of Burt's traps had been responsible for the deep wound? The more she thought of it, the more convinced she became that this was so. In a fight with another animal, surely there would have been some other signs of it, but his fur elsewhere was intact.

Tight-lipped, she washed her hands in warm water and dealt with the bread dough, which had risen to satisfactory roundness above the bowl's rim. Punching it to reduce its size became in her mind like punching Burt's self-assured face. Unfortunately, he couldn't be reduced in size the way the dough could.

Setting it for a final rise in the odd-shaped pan she had found, she eyed the portable oven tucked away

against the wall. She had never used such a thing in
her life before, and had no clear idea of how it
worked. Common sense told her that she would have
to set it directly on the stove top, but how in the
world could she regulate the fitful stove heat?

One thing was sure; the initial baking required a
high temperature, so she took wood from the dwindling pile and stacked it inside the gaping mouth of
the stove, leaving the front section open to generate a
draft.

"No, don't do that," she said sharply to the dog
when she noticed his teeth nibbling delicately at the
confining bandage, and immediately his ears fell
back to guilty flatness even as his tail thumped in-
gratiatingly on the wooden floor. Whoever owned
him, he had been well trained in polite behavior.

The cabin was filled with the tempting smell of
new-baked bread when Burt at last came back just as
dusk was falling over the clearing. Dani, seeking confidence for the battle she was sure would come, had
washed her face and hands and changed into a navy
linen dress that subtly outlined the most feminine of
her curves and intensified the blue of her eyes. The
makeup she had neglected the day before was applied
carefully to her reflection in the flyblown mirror
nailed to the wall over the sink, and she stared back
into its murky depths with satisfaction. Her brows
and eyelashes always looked better for the applica-
tion of pencil and mascara, although they were
several shades darker than the gold of her hair. Her
round cheeks took on a more sculptured shape with
the skillful use of rose-toned blusher, her lips a fuller

line from the deep pink of her favorite lipstick. She had all the confidence in the world for meeting the man she intended to tear into strips as she had torn the bandages that adorned the dog's wickedly injured paw.

The glow that lighted Burt's eyes from deep in their fathomless depths threw her off stroke for a moment or two. It was almost as if he had looked forward to coming back to her, to brandishing the fish strung loosely on a line suspended from his outstretched hand.

"Trout," he told her, his grin transforming serious features into a boyish replica of himself. "Have you ever tasted fresh-caught trout from a Chilcotin lake?" He breathed in deeply then and took his eyes from Dani to rest on the risen but misshapen loaf resting on the table. "You made bread?" he asked disbelievingly.

"Yes," she answered frigidly, picking up the knife she had placed in readiness and cutting into the still warm odd-shaped loaf. "I thought I'd better make something for us to eat in case you had the bad luck not to catch some innocent creature in your traps."

She gave him a fleeting glance before spreading the remains of the salmon paste on the thick slice cut from the loaf, and saw that the smile had faded from his face to be replaced by the more familiar set expression.

"You don't eat fish, either?" he queried dryly, accepting the bread she held out to him and biting deep into its crusty depths like a man too long deprived of the finer things in life. "This is fantastic," he mumbled through the mouthful, his eyes never leaving Dani's face. "You're not only beautiful, you can cook, too. Every man's dream," he ended on the note more familiar to her.

"Yes, I eat fish," she said frostily, ignoring the last part of his conversation. "I eat anything that's not caught in the kind of trap you seem to find necessary."

"I thought we'd been through all this last night," he said wearily, crossing to the counter and dropping the two good-sized fish into the bowl. "When it's a question of life or death—"

"Would you call the trapping and injuring of an innocent dog a matter of life or death?" Dani demanded fiercely, her eyes drawn, like Burt's, to the far side of the stove where a distinctive whine was heard.

"What are you talking about?" he asked aggressively, taking a step toward the indistinguishable mat of fur beside the stove. "Randy?" he exploded then, bending down quickly to the quiescent dog whose only movement was the rhythmic thumping of his tail against the wood floor. "What the hell are you doing here?"

"You know him?"

"Of course I know him," he returned abruptly without looking around at her. "He's—" He did turn his head then to say in a more controlled fashion, "He comes from Copper Canyon Ranch."

Dani stared at his blazing eyes through the fast-falling gloom. "You mean he's...Grant King's dog?"

"Yes."

She peered down at the dog, Randy, as he accepted the rough caress of a male hand down his sides, and he took on a different aspect. This dog knew Grant King, was part of his life, of the ranch life now directed by the man she had come all this way to see.

"What's happened to him?"

"Maybe you should go ask your traps!" Dani snapped.

The injured paw now lay on the broad palm of the man crouched down beside the dog. He looked around vaguely.

"What?"

"It was pretty obvious to me that his leg had been caught in one of your so-called humane traps," Dani flashed back. "He—"

"That's impossible," Burt interrupted brusquely, returning his attention to the animal, his expression shrouded in the dimming light.

"More impossible than the rabbit you brought home last night?" she demanded shrilly, oblivious, in the hysteria of the moment, to the intimate sound of "home." "What makes you think that a dog should be any more immune than the rabbit was?"

"Because Randy knows better than to—" Burt broke off abruptly and drew the kerosene lamp toward him as he straightened from the dog. "I can't see anything in this light."

Dani forbore to say anything while his broad, competent hand dealt with the lighting of the lamp, but when the cabin filled gradually with its glow she asked pointedly, "You know the dog well, then?"

With an irrritable shrug Burt crouched beside the animal again. "He comes over here now and then. Mostly when there's food around."

"That couldn't have been his reason today," Dani pointed out dryly. "There isn't enough food in this place to keep a mouse alive for too long!"

"I guess I'll leave his paw as it is for now," he said abstractedly, as if he hadn't heard her. With a final pat on the grateful head, he stood to his full height again and glanced at the barren stove top. "You didn't prepare any vegetables?"

"I wasn't to know what kind of prey you would be bringing back, was I?" she questioned stonily, meeting his level look with one of her own.

"No, I suppose you didn't," he returned evenly, then swiveled on his heeled boot to assess the contents of the upper-level cupboard. "Canned peas should be all right with fish, I guess, and some of that bread you made." He tossed the can down on the counter and bent his long legs to rummage in the lower cupboard and extract the inevitable frying pan.

Dani found, despite her genuine disgust with his food-finding practices, that her pulse gave a traitorous leap as her eyes fastened reluctantly on the powerful lines of his thighs, the hard flatness of his hips. Why couldn't he have been the kind of man who lived a normal life, the kind she could have taken home to her mother and introduced proudly? Instead, she could well imagine the scenario.

"Mom, this is Burt—I don't know what his last name is, but I love him very much. He lives in a tumbledown cabin way out in the Canadian wilderness. Why does he live there? Well, there was a little trouble where he worked in the States, and he thought it was better to leave and live in another country for a while.''

"Dani?"

Burt's puzzled question brought her back with a bump to reality. From the wary look in his eyes she surmised that it wasn't the first time he had spoken without her hearing.

"Where have you put the cooking oil?"

"Oh. It's—up there on the top shelf."

Her eyes followed the smooth ripple of his shoulder as he reached effortlessly up to the shelf and poured the oil sparingly into the frying pan in which he had placed the fish, which he must have cleaned away from the cabin. He really was self-sufficient, she reflected as she laid the table with knives and forks and wished briefly that there was butter for the bread she had made.

"How long have you lived here?" she asked abruptly, meeting his eyes as they turned from the stove.

"Quite a while," he said with casual finality, obviously not intending to elaborate.

But Dani felt like persisting. "You can't mean to stay here for the rest of your life. Don't you ever want to go back and see your family, your—" she paused delicately "—loved ones?"

"One day I will," he tossed lightly over his shoulder as he made a production of turning the sizzling fish and seasoning their upper halves.

"When the statute of limitations runs out?" she continued unabashedly.

"What do you know about the statute of limitations?" he turned to ask, an amused glint in his eyes reinforcing the mocking uplift of his strongly marked mouth.

"Nothing," she confessed without embarrassment. "Just that there's a time limit on how long a crime can be prosecuted."

His eyes took on a wary, withdrawn look. "Some crimes," he told her briefly, adding as he turned back to the cooking fish, "Will you open the can of peas and see to them?"

Dani hesitated momentarily, staring at his broad-shouldered back. Had his crime been so horrifying that the statute didn't apply to him? The fear that had filled her on her arrival at the cabin once more swept over her. He could be one of those homicidal maniacs who had prolonged periods of normality between their murderous bouts.

An attention-seeking whine from the dog distracted her. "What are we going to feed the dog?" she asked in what she hoped was a calm and possessed way as she went to open the can of peas.

"Mmm...." Burt looked speculatively at the tail-thumping animal. "There certainly isn't enough of this to share three ways."

"Maybe I can make him some porridge," Dani suggested as she tipped the peas into a saucepan. "I doubt if he's all that hungry right now with all that's happened to him today."

Burt at once picked up on her lightly stressed

criticism and said in sudden irritation, "I've told you it was no trap of mine that he got caught in. I'm not the only one in this area who's laid traps in the past few days."

"Well?"

"Well, what?"

"Should I make some cereal for. . . Randy?"

"You might as well," he conceded grudgingly, "although he's going to want a lot more than that tomorrow night."

Tomorrow night! Dani had a feeling that a lot of things could happen before tomorrow night, the least of which was what the dog would have on his diet.

Her brain worked busily while she automatically made a generous helping of porridge for the injured dog. If the animal had found his way here from Copper Canyon Ranch, then it must be possible for a human to take the reverse path. Fear had always been an alien concept to her—but then she had never run into anyone like Burt before. He was more manly than any man she had ever known before, more sexually attractive, but he was also the most mysterious man she had met. And fear did play the bigger part now in her wanting to get away.

Despite the trout's mouth-watering tastiness, Dani hardly noticed what she ate that night. Tension mounted by the minute as she sat across from Burt. It was as if he sensed the scheme she had in mind for getting to Copper Canyon Ranch, and the somber look in his eyes seemed to hold some kind of sad warning. Bread stuck in her throat when she suddenly realized that the last thing he would want was for her to reach someone who might take action on the basis of her suspicions.

As soon as their plates were cleared she jumped up and collected them, taking them to the counter then ladling water into a pan to heat for washing them.

"There isn't much water left," she said jerkily. "Is it much of a problem to get more?"

"Not in daylight," he retorted dryly. "Is there enough to last till morning?"

"Well—yes, I guess so." Enough for another coffee before bedtime, but none after that for personal washing. That reminded her of something else she had meant to investigate. "What do you do for baths?" she asked, turning back from the stove and resuming her chair.

"Baths?" He appeared to consider the matter thoughtfully, drawling lazily at last, "Well, there's the lake, but that's a mite cold at this time of the year for somebody from the sunny state of California. But there's always the old washtub."

"Washtub?" she repeated faintly.

"Didn't you see it while you were...looking around?"

She shook her head, eyeing him suspiciously.

"It's a lot more civilized than it seems." Burt had lost his intense look and was now evidently finding it hard not to smile too widely. "What could be cozier than tubbing yourself right in front of a hot stove?" His eyes went speculatively over what he could see of her. "You shouldn't have to fold yourself up too much."

"I don't intend to fold myself up at all!" she

snapped, getting up and snatching the warmed water from the stove. "I'll wait till I get to the ranch—I'm sure they'll have at least a shower there."

"I wouldn't be surprised," he shrugged. "It seems to be quite a fancy place."

"You haven't been there?" Suspicion reared its head again. "I thought you said you knew my grandfather."

"I did," he returned evenly, "but it was mostly here that I met him. As I told you before, he judged a man as he found him."

Dani put the pan back on the stove and sat down again, glancing wonderingly around the room. "My grandfather came here?"

"Quite a lot. In fact, we often played crib with that board and pack of cards we used last night."

Dani gave a little shiver and rested her chin on her hands. "I feel I should have sensed that somehow," she confessed softly, "but then I never knew him. Strange, isn't it, that you knew him so well and I didn't know him at all?"

"That's the way it happens sometimes. Two of my grandparents died before I was born."

"Will you tell me about my grandfather?" she asked hesitantly. "Mom knew him only through his letters, and dad hardly ever talked about him. Of course, dad didn't know him very well, either. After my grandmother died, dad was sent to live with his aunt in California. She really brought him up."

"Did your mother write often to him?"

"No." Dani laughed softly. "I think she'd have written a lot more if he hadn't been—well, such an important man. She wrote to tell him about dad's dying, and she actually cried when he sent a letter back saying he couldn't send us any money because his capital was all tied up in stock." She blinked rapidly at the tears threatening to spill over. "That wasn't why she had written him; she just wanted to feel closer to dad's one remaining relative."

Burt rose and refilled their coffee cups—whether it was to give her time to recover herself or not, Dani wasn't sure, but she gave him a watery smile when he straightened up. Where had all her fear gone suddenly? It seemed to have dissipated as quickly as the anger that had filled her not long ago when she had thought Randy's wound was caused by one of his traps.

Maybe it was because she was still suspended in an enchanted state between reality and fantasy, a no-man's-land where there was nothing strange about sitting like this in marriagelike intimacy with a man she had known only for days.

"Your grandfather, whatever his financial standing, *was* an important man," Burt said slowly, stirring his coffee although he had put no sugar in it, "in the way he lived and—" he shrugged "—in his philosophy of life, I guess. He...cared a lot about anything living, human, beast or bird." A wry smile touched the corner of his mouth. "I suppose you'd call him one of nature's gentlemen. He trusted everybody, and everybody in turn trusted him."

Some of the animated interest died out of Dani's eyes. "Maybe he didn't always trust wisely," she said, her voice tart. "Grant King's case, for instance."

Burt sighed, but not impatiently. "I don't know anything about that," he said quietly, "but I do know that Hank Benson would never have wanted his granddaughter to go through with something like this on her own."

"Then he should have thought of that and provided for us!" she snapped irritably, pushing back her chair and pacing up and down the small room. Her steps slowed and stopped as a thought hit her. "You're a lawyer, Burt, you could help me."

He looked up, wrinkling his tanned brow above flaring eyes. "I don't practice law anymore," he reminded her harshly. "I couldn't fight a case for my own mother, even if I wanted to."

"But you wouldn't have to," Dani said eagerly, sitting again and propping her elbows on the table as she looked across it. "Don't you see, you could just advise me, privately; nobody else would need to know. And if—if you told me I wouldn't stand a chance, I'd listen to you."

"Good. Then I'll tell you right now that you would never stand a chance against a man like Grant King. He wields a lot of power in these parts, and no local lawyer would go against him to that extent."

"Then I'll go to Vancouver!" she cried. "There must be people there who aren't scared to death of him."

"Do you have that kind of money?" he gibed, frowning as he took in her implication that he was numbered in her mind as one of the fearful ones.

Her eyes dropped. "I—"

"I thought not," he interrupted dryly.

Dani was dangerously near to tears. "What am I supposed to do, then?" she gulped. "Go back home and forget that my grandfather worked for years to benefit somebody else?"

Unexpectedly he stretched a hand across the table and lifted her chin gently with his fingers. "You could stay here with me for a while."

Her eyes snapped open and widened incredulously as they searched his face to catch a trace of humor. There was none. Jerking her chin away from his fingers, she stood up and glared down into his intent black eyes.

"What do you think I am?" she asked thickly. "Like most other men, you think because I work as a model I'm up for grabs. Well, I'm not, Mr.—oh!" She waved her hands in irritation at not even knowing what name to call him. "And even if I were there's nothing about you that would interest me."

"No?"

She watched warily as he rose lightly to his feet and came around the table to stand close to her.

"That wasn't the impression I got yesterday." His hand touched her face again, his fingers brushing lightly over her cheek before his thumb rested close to her eye. "Who did you make yourself beautiful for tonight? Randy?"

Her eyes went involuntarily to where the dog lay with his head between front paws, breathing heavily as he slept.

"Maybe you're the one who should have that

name!'' she scorned. ''But I'm not about to be used by you because you h-haven't seen a woman in a while!''

A flicker of his dark eyes showed that he had taken her meaning, but it obviously made no dent in his maddening assurance.

''What is there to stop me doing whatever I like with you?''

CHAPTER FIVE

DANI RAN HER TONGUE over her lips before whispering dryly, "You wouldn't dare."

"You think not?" His hand spanned the short distance between them and curved around her waist to press her toward him. Even if she hadn't been numbed with shock she could have done nothing about the underlying force of steel in his arm.

But she was numb, her eyes showing a flicker of fear as her body touched the hardness of male muscle and flesh, knowing fleetingly that her earlier premonition had been justified. Borne in on her subconscious, too, was the knowledge that he was right. There wasn't a thing she could do if he decided that his need for a woman overrode the civilized instincts he must have once possessed.

"Wh-why are you being like th-this now?" she stammered, blue eyes pleading against the mocking glow deep in his, but jerking her face away from the gentle exploration his fingers were making of her skin.

His hand lost its gentleness and grasped her chin, pulling her head around and up so that her eyes were forced to stare into his.

"You're not flattering my male ego much if you're

saying you've forgotten that little scene yesterday,"
he gibed harshly. "Let's just say it reminded me of
how much I've been missing lately." His hand slid
around to caress her nape. "You'll just have to
forgive me if I'm a little rougher than the men you're
used to. Skills get rusty when they're not used."

Dani pulled in a deep, shaky breath. "I'm not—
not used to men in the way you mean. I—I've
never—" She broke off and bit the soft part of her
underlip.

"You expect me to believe that?"

"I don't care if you believe me or not," she flared,
the soft touch of his fingers massaging gently at the
back of her head stinging her nerve ends into vibrant
life again. "It's true, whatever you think."

"There's one sure way to find out," he suggested
with narrowed eyes and jerked her against him, the
impact taking the breath from her body so that the
firm hand he held at her back was totally unnecessary
to hold her there.

"Please—" she leaned bonelessly against him,
knowing that without his support she would fall ig-
nominiously to the floor "—don't do this."

She saw the flash of his strong teeth as he bent his
head until his mouth was a bare inch from hers.

"No?" His hand slid up through her hair to lift her
head higher. "You liked this yesterday." The dry
warmth of his lips touched hers lightly, more than
once, teasing at the corners before settling forcefully
over them to part their softly compressed line.

When her resistance held and firmed he resorted to
the even more deadly tactic of running the tip of his

tongue lightly, suggestively, across the sensitive surface of her mouth and, when she gasped, taking devastatingly complete possession. Her mind grew dizzy as it tried to cope with the urgent messages sent to it from her plundered mouth and the shocking awareness of his arousal as his hands slid down over her lightly covered rib cage and curved around her hips, pressing her to the uncompromising hardness of his thighs.

"No...oh, no..." she moaned when his mouth lifted slightly and went hotly across her skin to nibble her ear and the sensitive cord leading from it.

"You're beautiful," he murmured jerkily against her neck, his eyes heavy lidded as he drew back to look feverishly into the misted blue of her eyes. "I've waited for you for a long time...too long."

Dani's eyes went from the black glitter in his to the bloodred of his mouth, then back again. "You didn't know me," she whispered.

"But I knew you'd come."

Her—or somebody else? Would it have mattered to him which woman had stumbled into his retreat? Strangely, it didn't matter to Dani suddenly. Her only awareness was of his whip-lean figure pressed to hers, the magic power his lips possessed to transport her to a dimension unknown to her before. It was a continuation of the unreal world that had surrounded her for the past few days, a world in which Burt, not Grant King, took complete precedence.

"Will you stay?"

She blinked against the eyes looming above her, black eyes gleaming with small flecks of light. Above her...momentary panic rustled through her when she felt the hard, unyielding mattress of the bunk beneath her, the heavy pressure of Burt's body above her.

"What!" she breathed, trying—and failing—to assimilate all the impressions, physical and emotional, that crowded in on her.

"Will you stay here, with me?"

His voice seemed to come from a distance, a distance that spanned all that had been and all that might be. How could she stay here when her mother waited for her in California, when she had to press on to Copper Canyon Ranch and Grant King? Even if she had wanted to....

"Burt, I can't."

More eloquent than any words of his might have been was the upward sweep of his hand, the firm but provocative cupping of a breast now bared to his touch, the evocative feelings that flooded and drowned her.

"Will you stay, Dani?" he persisted huskily, pressing his mouth to the soft roundness that firmed under the probe of his seeking lips. "Say it, Dani, just once."

"No." She shook her head negatively on the pillow, rebelling more against her own overwhelming desire to submit than his to force her. The lucid part of her mind monitored the situation and found it ludicrous. Was it possibly Dani Benson lying here on a rough bunk in the wilderness, imprisoned by a man's heavy weight, actually fighting her own impulse to savor the experience all too many men would have been willing to share in her recent past?

What was so different about this man? Or was it that very difference that blotted out all her past inhibitions, making her devastatingly conscious of his primitive male attraction? Her hands were conscious of it in the smooth, hard texture of his muscled flesh, her heart aware of it in the increased pumping of heated blood through her veins, and now only her conscious thoughts remained as a fragile barrier.

Even that slight defense crumbled when Burt's lips outlined a more determined onslaught on her physical senses, her fair skin burning where his rough chin grazed as he kissed the soft hollows in her throat and shoulders, the taut swell of her breasts. A strangled sob escaped her as her hands cupped the sides of his face and raised it to the trembling readiness of her lips.

"All right, damn you," she breathed shakily, "I'll stay."

Whatever she had expected, it wasn't the immediate withdrawal she sensed in him, a slackening of the passion that had ignited hers and left her aching for some unknown fulfillment. It was nothing physical; he was still as close to her as before, so close that she could have reached up easily to touch the lips she craved on hers. But the gap between them might as well have stretched a thousand miles.

"You're sure?" The husky depth of his voice was even more shaky than her own had been, and Dani looked questioningly into the dark eyes that blazed intently into the misted blue of hers.

"I . . . think so. I've . . . never felt this way before."

His hand left the curve of her throat and stroked gently, almost thoughtfully, along the soft strands of her hair fanned out against the pillow.

"There's no hurry," he said slowly, his eyes on the movement of his hand. "We can wait until you're sure."

Irritation, born of the unfulfilled fires he had kindled, swept through Dani like a storm. What did he want from her? He had kissed and caressed her into a state of mindless acquiescence, and now he was telling her that he could wait for her final capitulation.

She opened her mouth to protest, but the words were stifled in her throat when Burt groaned and slid his hand under her nape, pulling her head up to meet the fierce demand of his questing mouth. Anger seeped away in the renewed desire his lips brought to vibrant life.

An apologetic yelp from the door went jarringly through their bodies, which seemed as one as they kissed and clung and explored each other with the wonder of newness. Burt's hair brushed Dani's cheek as he turned his head to survey the abject Randy. Then with an explosive sigh he turned back to smile wryly into Dani's eyes.

"Saved by the dog," he grimaced, but Dani sensed, as he rolled from her and stood upright, that he felt more than a little relief at Randy's innocent disruption of the scene taking place on the bunk.

She watched his wide-framed figure stride across the floor to the door, his dark-skinned hands reaching around to tuck the loose ends of his shirt into the waistband of his work pants, and shame mingled with astonishment as warm color washed over her.

Relieved that Burt had accompanied the dog on his outdoor mission, she slid off the bunk and adjusted her dress with trembling fingers. She must have been crazy, she told herself as she searched feverishly in her bag for a comb, then drew it randomly through her tangled hair. Never, never, never had she allowed a man to make love to her like that, let him touch her in that intimate way, or draw that kind of response from her.

A fleeting acknowledgment crossed her mind that neither had she ever met a man of Burt's caliber who was capable of sweeping aside the inhibitions that had become part of her.

Shivering despite the warmth in the room, she went to stand before the stove, gazing sightlessly down into it as she pressed the comb against her mouth. What had she done? There was no way she could stay here with him as she had told him she would. He had been crazy to suggest it, and she had been stupid to let him think she would go along with his craziness. She had to think of some way, any way, to get out of here.

Before she had time to do any more than form the resolution, however, the door handle rattled and Burt came in, followed by the limping dog. Dani gave one quick look over her shoulder and turned back to the stove, not wanting to see the glow of anticipation that lighted the back of Burt's eyes. A glow she had unwittingly put there.

"You'll need your coat on for going outside," Burt said quietly to her taut back. "It's cool out there."

He was already holding her raincoat when she went to the door, and after she slid her arms into it he picked up the flashlight from the dresser.

"I'll...manage alone, thanks," she said without looking at him, and he hesitated for only a moment before handing over the flashlight. His eyes were still on her broodingly as she closed the door behind her.

She leaned against the door, her eyes becoming accustomed to the darkness. Far above, stars more brilliant than any she had ever noticed sparkled under their navy canopy. A fierce rush of homesickness washed over her. What was she doing here, far from everyone and everything that was familiar to her? The thought of her mother's gently loving face, with its lines of pain etched deeply into her soft skin, brought a hard lump into Dani's throat. How could she have forgotten her reason for being here, even for one minute?

Switching on the flashlight, she moved off, carefully averting her eyes from the cozy glow falling from the cabin window. She didn't want to see Burt now, she didn't ever want to see him again. In these surroundings he held the power of mystery in his hands, the romantic attraction of novelty, even the stirring of compassion in her heart for his predicament, although it was brought about by himself. In her own environment she would probably have seen him for the man he really was, a cowardly fugitive from the society whose laws he had broken.

Returning to the cabin, she was drawn to the pool of light that fell in a square in front of her. Her eyes seemed haunted as she stared in and saw Burt, his long body bent as he attended to the stove for the night, mucles moving supplely under his shirt as his arms moved forward and back. Fear licked along her veins when her eyes rested on the grimly powerful line of his profile. If he decided to spend the night with her in the bunk she would be powerless to stop him.

He straightened from the stove as she pushed open the door and stood with her back to it, eyeing him fearfully when his boots tapped their tattoo toward her.

"What's wrong?" he asked softly, taking the coat from her lifeless arms and turning back to pull her gently to him when he had deposited it on the peg. "You look as if you think I'm about to swallow you whole."

When she made no answer, he tilted her chin up until her eyes met the level hardness in his. "I told you there's no hurry. Are you afraid I'll throw you down and rape you?"

Conscious of his big hands resting heavily on her narrow waist, she could only nod dumbly, and immediately felt the tightening of his fingers on her chin.

"You think there's going to be a need for that?"

Dani shook her head and whispered, "I...I don't know."

"Then let me reassure you," he said caustically, bending his head as he pulled her farther into his arms. Against her lips he muttered almost savagely, "Before two more days have gone by you'll be begging me to make love to you."

The arrogance of his statement was lost on Dani as she struggled to maintain the control she knew was sliding out of her hands when his mouth parted the unresisting outlines of hers and bruised their soft surfaces with kisses that had less to do with love than with a savage desire to hurt. What made her fear more palpable was the rise, however reluctant, of her own matching savagery in the response of her lips, the unmistakable arch of her body to the taut bow of his.

Once again it was Burt who exerted the pressure that set them apart. Breathing raggedly, his eyes flashed down into Dani's.

"See what I mean?" he snatched breath to say, dropping his hands from her and stepping back, though his eyes still drew her to him like a magnet. "Go to bed, Dani, and sleep in peace. I won't disturb you." He turned abruptly and went into his own room, banging the door behind him.

Dani was still far from sleeping in peace hours later, as she twisted and turned on the narrow bunk. Ironically, it wasn't Burt she feared so much now as her own unprecedented reactions to the sheer physical presence of him. Without thinking twice about it, she knew that every one of the models she knew at the agency would have succumbed even quicker than she had to Burt's overwhelming masculinity. Superb male specimens like him rarely showed up in Los Angeles, apart from the occasional movie

or television star who cultivated the masculine image
with a zeal that amounted to fetish. But there was
nothing contrived about Burt. He was what he was,
take him or leave him.

And Dani had to leave him. She had never had
much in common with the girls she met in modeling.
Away from their normal hometown environment
they had a freeness from responsibility that she had
never known since her father's death. Marsha was a
constant weight around her neck, however lovingly
Dani bore the burden. Her mother needed her...
needed the financial freedom Grant King could give
her.

Randy sighed in his corner by the stove, and a sudden thought filled Dani's mind. If the dog had found
his way here from Copper Canyon Ranch he could
find his way back again. She had thought of it
before, but now the idea had taken on an added
urgency. The black and white sheep dog sleeping by
the stove could turn out to be her salvation. Tomorrow she would. . . .

BUT RANDY WAS STILL far from up to the long journey to the ranch the following morning. As usual,
Burt had gone when Dani woke to a bright new
morning, and the dog was nowhere visible until she
had washed and dressed and drunk two cups of
the coffee Burt had left warming on the stove. Then
she saw him, lying full length under the high shade of
the pines, head lifting when he heard the cabin door
open. But he made no more effort than the raising of
a faintly wagging tail at Dani's appearance.

Crossing the bed of pine needles, Dani dropped to her knees beside the dog and fondled his silky ears. "Oh, Randy," she said wistfully, "I wish you could take me to your master. I can't stay here much longer." Her eyes went from arching pines with their strong, straight trunks to the roughly cleared area in front of the cabin, resting finally on the cabin itself.

It had a stark kind of beauty, she had to admit, a quiet stillnesss apart from the bird song that might appeal to a city man as a weekend retreat. But to a professional like Burt, used to the varied cultural attractions a city such as Boston had to offer, it must seem like a primeval prison.

The morning dragged, although she attempted to spin out the hours with the chores that should have taken minutes. Finally, with a sigh, she decided to complete the scouring of the cabin by turning out the cupboards above and below the sink counter.

Ecstatic yelps heralded an arrival just before noon and Dani rose stiffly to her feet, conscious suddenly of her disheveled appearance. If the unexpected visitor turned out to be Grant King, come in search of his dog, what kind of impression would she make on him with her hair tumbling chaotically around her unmade-up face, and dirt smudges, she saw from a hasty glance into the fly-specked mirror, adorning her nose and cheeks?

Hastily she smoothed her hair and scrubbed the dust from her face with her fingers before walking to the open door, arranging her features into what she hoped was a polite but businesslike appearance.

The sun's brilliance blinded her after the dimness

inside the cabin, and she called to the hazily discerned figure approaching from the edge of the clearing, "Hello, who is it?" only then shading her eyes with her hand.

"Who were you expecting?" Burt's deep voice countered, and she sagged weakly against the door frame. Relief mingled with an odd kind of pleasure in knowing it was Burt, not Grant King, who had broken the stillness of this secret place.

"I—I thought it might be Grant King," she rallied her strength to say as Burt lounged into her clear view.

"Oh?" His fingers brushed lightly against a smudge she had missed low down on her cheek. "I doubt if you would have got far with him, looking as if you're an overworked housewife instead of a cool, collected model lady from California."

"What I look like won't matter when I see Grant King." She jerked her face away from his lingering fingertips and stepped backward into the cabin. "What are you doing home so early?" she demanded, realizing too late that she had implied an intimacy she had no intention of backing up.

"I brought something for the dog to eat," he drawled, turning his head to look at Randy, who was greedily devouring a horrifying mass of bloody meat. "And something for us," he added tongue in cheek, bringing up his free hand and flourishing what looked like a roast cut from an all too recently living animal.

Dani took a further step back into the dim room,

her eyes widening in horror when she saw the glistening red of the cut surface.

"How could you think of eating something like that?" she choked, dragging her eyes from the mutilated membranes to Burt's impassively set face.

"It's no different from what you eat normally in California," he shrugged, adding with mocking emphasis as he carried the portion of red flesh past her, "It's just a little fresher, that's all."

Her eyes were still filled with the repugnance she felt when he finished preparing the meat for roasting, placing it in a large-sized oven pan he found among the cupboard contents she had strewed across the floor while she cleaned.

"Now how about some lunch?" he asked in a cheerful voice that set her teeth on edge."

"How about iced melon and chicken in aspic?" she scorned, turning disgustedly back to the doorway and lifting a weary hand to the moist nape of her neck. "You know very well there's nothing for lunch today, any more than there was yesterday or the day before."

"There's the bread you baked yesterday," he suggested as he left the stove area and came to stand next to her, making her uncomfortably conscious of his male closeness, too aware of the potent scent of his shaving cologne, which she had picked up and handled for a moment before setting it down beside all the other paraphernalia on the sink counter.

"Big deal," she jeered without looking at him. "Should we have some farm-fresh butter with it? Or maybe some—"

"Cheese?" he cut in, giving her a smiling sidelong glance.

Dani searched his face for signs of double-dealing. "Cheese?" she echoed disbelievingly.

"Put some coffee on, and I'll bring it in."

She stared thoughtfully after his jaunty figure as he left the cabin, and slowly set about making the coffee he had ordered. Where would he have found cheese in a place like this?

It was only later, when they were sharing the thick slices of bread and dark yellow, creamy cheese, that Burt elaborated.

"It's made in the old-fashioned way by one of the farm wives in the area," he explained while munching heartily on the healthy bread and cheese combination. "She usually gives me some of her newest batch."

I'll bet she does, Dani thought involuntarily, picturing his effect on an isolated farm wife with little company but her husband's, who might not appreciate her domestic skills as much as a half-starved Burt would. But she kept that thought to herself, saying casually instead, "Does she live far from here?"

"Far enough," he responded just as casually, but the narrowed set of his eyes told her that he hadn't missed her implication that where there was a woman dispensing cheese there must be an outlet to the outside world.

But the possibility of reaching that outside world receded as, biting into the tangy cheese and thick bread, Dani fed the hunger that seemed to have gnawed into her since her arrival at the cabin. Food

had never tasted so good...but then she had never
been this hungry before, even in the days when she
had to watch her diet carefully because every extra
ounce was exaggerated by the television cameras.
Strange, she mused, how that part of her life already
seemed far in the past. Some fatalistic instinct told
her that she would never go back to it, even if Grant
King couldn't be persuaded to part with the share she
and her mother were entitled to in the ranch. There
must be some other kind of work she could do while
training at night for an office job, which would be
enough to support them but not, she sighed, to provide the treatments Marsha needed.

"What's worrying you?" Burt broke into her
thoughts.

"What? Oh," she shrugged, pushing her hair
behind her ear at one side, "just...things.

"Things?"

A frown of irritation marred her smooth forehead.
"Yes, things!" she snapped. "You don't think I can
just disappear from the world without trace and have
no one worry about me, do you? Unlike you, it
seems," she ended sarcastically.

His mouth quirked at the corners as if he meant to
smile, but his voice was serious when he spoke.
"Your mother won't be worrying about you. The—"

"How can you possibly know that?" she cut in
sharply. "She'll have called Grant King by now and
found out that I haven't contacted him yet."

"No, she won't have." He shook his head with
maddening surety and cut off another slab of bread
before going on, "The phone lines are down, so if

she tried to call the ranch she'd know that you couldn't get through to her, either. So—" he broke off a healthy chunk of cheese and placed it on the bread "—she'll assume that you arrived safely."

"The lines won't be down forever." Dani's hand trembled as she picked up her bread and cheese, then replaced it before it reached her mouth.

"True," he said laconically between bites, "but it could take a while. Long enough for—for you to make up your mind that fighting King is a losing proposition, and to go back where you belong," One black brow quirked up as a lazy gleam came into his eyes. "Meanwhile you could brighten my life considerably." His gaze went appreciatively around the room she had cleaned. "You've already made me aware of how much a man needs a woman around the place."

"I didn't do it for your sake," she lashed out, her eyes sparkling frostily across the table. "I'd have gone mad stuck out here with nothing to do, so don't flatter yourself." Her eyes narrowed dangerously. "And I've no intention of going home without settling things at Copper Canyon Ranch. Your opinion of my chances doesn't interest me."

Burt's jaw clamped down once, then he lifted his coffee mug to drain it before getting to his feet. "Please yourself," he shrugged, moving off to the door. "Right now I have work to do."

"Are you...leaving again?" she said with hopeful hesitancy to his back. Perhaps Randy, after his long rest and the meal Burt had brought back for him, could be persuaded to take the homeward trip to the ranch that afternoon. By nightfall, when Burt returned, she could be miles away, maybe even at her goal. Her heart sank when he turned back with a mocking smile, as if he had guessed her intentions.

"The work I have to do is around here," he said complacently, "or hadn't you noticed that we're getting low on firewood?"

"There's a stack of it at the side of the cabin," she reminded him pointedly, and he shook his head.

"What seems like a stack to you is only a few days' supply," he told her blandly, "and I'd sure like more of that bread you bake."

"I won't be here that long."

He hesitated fractionally before taking a step or two back into the room. "I think I might be able to persuade you otherwise," he said with deliberate huskiness, and Dani put the width of the table between them.

"Don't touch me," she warned, her hand fastening around the handle of the sharp knife they had used to slice the bread and cheese, lifting it menacingly when he gave a low laugh and came straight to her.

"You're scaring me to death," he jeered, coming to a lazy halt at her side. "Come on, show me how vicious you can be. My heart's about here, I think." He laid a big hand to left of center on his wide chest and mocked her with his eyes. "Go ahead, I won't stop you."

Blue eyes sparkled angrily into mocking dark ones as Dani's hand tightened to whiteness on the knife. Moments seemed like ages as they stared at each other, until at last the mockery died from Burt's eyes to be replaced by something far more intense. As if sensing the calming of the turbulence in her, too, he reached up a hand and took the knife from hers, laying it down behind him without shifting his eyes.

Then his hands were on her hips, drawing her to him slowly, and she had no strength to resist. The touch of his mouth on hers was feather light and warm, so warm that her lips parted without urging from him, knowing from the quick firming of his lips that the unconscious gesture had excited him instantly, surely.

Her hands slid up to rest momentarily on the spot where his heart jumped erratically in his chest, then continued up to clutch briefly at his shoulders before her arms twined around his neck, her body arching to the curve of his in willing compliance with his hands. She seemed to be absorbed into his strength and made part of him, as if she had lived all of her life for this moment. Her thighs accepted the hard pressure against them as if nothing in the world could be more natural than this basic urge that drove them together, desire lending experience to Dani's lips and hands as she returned Burt's kisses, his caresses that had all the surety of knowledge.

The abruptness with which Burt put her from him left her shaking, her eyes misty as she blinked uncomprehendingly into the blurred outline of his hardset face.

"Burt?" she whispered.

"Dear God, Dani, what do you think I'm made of?" he said tersely, the tips of his fingers gouging deeply into the soft flesh of her arms. "I'd better get out of here right now or I won't be responsible for the consequences.''

"Consequences?" she asked dazedly, her eyes clinging to the firm outline of his mouth. "What consequences?"

"Do I really have to spell them out?" he answered with another question, grimly put. "You may be as innocent as you look, but I doubt if you're that naive."

A flood of understanding cleared the brain cells that had been inactive for the past few minutes, and Dani turned away, embarrassed, from his leavy-lidded stare.

"Get out of here," she muttered thickly, not stopping to think that she was ordering him from his own home. "Just get out of here."

"Don't worry, I'm going," he retorted, and she heard the tapping tread of his boot heels across the floor. "Right now I need a cold douse in the lake."

Dani stood with her hands twisted painfully together for a long time after he had gone. What was there about him that made her forget all the tenets of her fastidious upbringing? It was as if he had the power to transport her to another place, another dimension, in which the moral sense of a lifetime melted into nothingness when compared to the sensual feelings he could incite in her . . . sensual feelings she had guessed at possessing, but had been content to wait for the right man to bring to fruition.

And Burt Whatever-his-name-was could never be that man. The prospect of living in exile from everyone and everything dear to her was one that had no appeal whatsoever. Even if she loved him.... She dropped into her chair at one side of the rough table.

Love was something that grew between two people, blossoming in the fullness of time to a deep need to spend the rest of life with each other, to share the upbringing of the children they would create together from their love. Her eyes lifted heavily and went around the starkly primitive room. What hopes could there be here for a normal family life, even if...?

She rose quickly and went to the cupboard in which the pans were stored, taking out the two largest and dipping water into them. At least the physical action of washing her hair would keep at bay the useless dreams filling her mind.

Later, her hair hanging in wet strands, she carried a chair outside to a sunny spot. Her eyes went involuntarily to where Burt, stripped to the waist, wielded a glistening ax on the pile of wood awaiting his attention. Her eyes flickered once over the bronzed torso with its rippling muscles as Burt systematically split the wood for the stove, then she gave herself up to the hot sun, closing her eyes as she lifted her face to its warming glow. By every precedent she knew, a sun this warm rated a lounger by a pool, a bikini exposing as much of her body as possible to its tanning rays.

"Dani? Wake up. I've brought you some coffee."

The painful crick in her neck told her she must have fallen asleep, and her lids blinked fitfully as she took in her surroundings. There was the close press of overhanging trees, the cleared area with its protruding tree stumps, the round bole of a sawed-off tree where Burt had scattered creamy chips from his chopping. Her eyes went farther up and looked blankly into the darkest pair of eyes she had ever seen.

"Oh," she said without emotion, "it's you."

"It's me," he returned unequivocally. "As soon as you've drunk your coffee you can take your bath."

"Bath?"

"Bath," he confirmed, folding his long body until he sat near her chair, then handing her the faintly steaming coffee mug. "I've split enough wood to last for a week or two."

"Bully for you," she responded, her voice weakly acid. The thought that she wouldn't be here to be warmed by the neatly stacked wood wasn't entirely pleasurable. Why couldn't Burt have been an ordinary, everyday man she might have met in California? The kind of man she could have taken home to meet her mother? Marsha would like him, she reflected, still half dozing in the sun, almost oblivious to the silent figure at her side. Her mother would have sensed that Burt had the power to stir her daughter to the depths of her romantic soul, but even Marsha would have reservations about a man who found it necessary to hide himself away from the life he had known, the family who cared about him.

"What will you do when you go back home?"

A stab of irritation brought Dani into a more upright position. "I'll find a job of some kind," she said coolly, taking a sip of the lukewarm coffee and setting it back on her knee.

"Not modeling?"

"I'm tired of that." She frowned at a tree on the far side of the clearing. "Maybe I'll try office work for a while...who knows? Or—" she shot him a sideways glance "—I might help Grant King run the ranch. My mother could come and live there, too, after—after she's packed up in California." Her eyes drifted around the encircling trees, noting the new green growth. "She would like it here."

"Would she?" The question seemed innocuous enough, but there was a tautening of his voice when he went on, "How about you? Do you like it here?"

"Me? I'm a city girl, born and bred." She smiled in self-mockery as she indicated the dog stretched out on Burt's far side. "I even thought Randy was a coyote or some other wild creature."

"But you coped with his wound," Burt pointed out, turning as if reminded to run his strong fingers over the muddy-looking bandage, murmuring soothingly to the dog as he exposed the injury. "Clean as a whistle...but maybe we should leave it open to the air and Randy's tongue now."

The partially healed gash made Dani feel nauseous again, and she turned her head away as she said tightly, "People should be put in jail for setting traps like that. How can they sleep at night knowing some poor animal is going crazy trying to get free of them?"

"Trapping is a way of life for some people," he said shortly, laying the dog's paw gently down before caressing the black ears.

Like you, Dani wondered silently as he rose and stretched his long limbs, more overpoweringly masculine than any male she had ever known. The thought involuntarily crossed her mind that it was a criminal waste of the talents he obviously possessed for him to spend his waking moments involved in a never ending battle to survive in the wilderness. She knew without questioning the thought that he must have been a brilliant lawyer, concise in his judgments and dedicated to hard work.

"Why did you do it?" she asked suddenly, knowing from the telltale widening of his eyes as his head swiveled down to look at her that he was even more surprised than she herself at the tack her thoughts had taken.

"Do what?" The familiar mocking gleam took the sober look from his eyes. "I'm thirty-one years old, so there are quite a few things I could regret having done. What, particularly, did you have in mind?"

Dani raised a sheltering hand over her eyes and looked up at his closed expression. "The reason you came here," she said with more confidence than she felt. "Couldn't you go back and—"

"I can never go back," he said, so harshly that she shrank visibly from his vehemence. "Our experiences shape us," he went on more coolly, even returning to the mocking stance he adopted so often, his eyes dropping to the clear outline of her curves in soft white cotton T-shirt, "just as you'll find this experience with a wild man of the woods has shaped you."

That was a thought that could bear repeating, Dani thought confusedly as she dragged her gaze away from the black eyes that seemed to draw her hypnotically. Her life in California, even her mother,

seemed far away in this remote clearing surrounded
by the stillness of ages. It *did* seem like an enchanted world to her, a world dominated by a man
with forceful chin and shoulders, a man who had
plumbed the secret depths of her and left her curious
about the final oneness a man and a woman could
share. In that strange half-world in which she had
been living for the past few days, it seemed natural
and right that she should know the outlines of the
male body standing close to her chair, the power she
possessed to rouse him to the same kind of passion he
inspired in her.

But sensing the reality that would descend on her
mesmerized senses during the next day or so, Dani
composed her voice as she said, "I doubt if I'll even
remember him once I'm away from this place. It's
like a holiday romance, you know?" She squinted up
at him with as much mockery as he had shown to her.
"Important at the time, but hard to recall when
you're back to reality."

His hard jawline contracted momentarily, but then
he held an uncompromising hand down to her.
"Your bath's ready."

Her hand lifted without her volition and was
clasped in the encompassing bigness of his. But once
on her feet, she pulled it free as if his touch stung
her.

"I'll wait until I reach civilization," she said shortly.

The black brows lifted in a maddening arch. "And
here was I thinking you were a fastidious lady concerned about her cleanliness. Civilization doesn't

look too kindly on unwashed bodies, even if this par-
ticular one is . . . beautiful.''

Only the knowledge that what he had said was
true, however crudely put, forced Dani's steps
toward the cabin. A bath in warm soapy water would
go a long way toward giving her the necessary confidence to face Grant King the next day. And she was
determined that, one way or the other, she would
make it to Copper Canyon Ranch or die in the attempt.

Burt followed her into the cabin and, while she
stared in horrified fascination at the round wooden
tub placed directly in front of the stove, strode forward to busy himself taking steaming buckets and
pans from the stove top and pouring them into the
washtub in streaming cascades.

CHAPTER SIX

"SORRY I CAN'T PROVIDE any bath bubbles," Burt said with a trace of sarcasm, his boots sounding loud against the floorboards as he came toward her. "That's something you'll have to wait for until you reach civilization."

Scarcely hearing him, Dani looked from the steaming tub to his overlarge figure, which dominated the room. "I...I'm not about to take a bath with—in these conditions," she amended belatedly, knowing from his wickedly perceptive look that he was entirely aware of what she had meant to say.

"Don't worry," he said, sounding amused as he moved off toward the door, "I won't peek. Even Randy will keep his male distance. Unless, of course—" he cocked an amused brow at her from the door "—you feel the need of assistance in scrubbing your back. Randy might be a little rough, but I think I can guarantee...satisfaction."

With that he went noisily from the cabin while Dani looked enigmatically after him. Satisfaction...yes, he would always offer that, and deliver it, to a woman. But not this woman, she told herself determinedly, stepping forward to look into the half-filled tub. The thought of being clean all over super-

seded any qualms she might have harbored about
Burt's possible invasion of her privacy, and in
another moment she was stripping off the clothes she
had worn all day, then stepping into the round tub
with its two iron hoops encircling it to ensure water-
tightness.

Once she had figured out a way to sit in the tub,
her knees folded in a partial arc, she gave herself up
to the pure sensuousness of relaxing warmth from the
heated water. It had been good of Burt, she reflected,
to go to the trouble of providing for her what must
seem a luxury to him. He had mentioned earlier that
the lake, despite or because of its coldness, was bath
enough for him, but she was grateful for the warmth
bathing her own lower parts and sending a corre-
sponding glow of well-being to the rest of her.

It was only later, when she stretched out a seeking
hand for the soap that would normally be at arm's
reach, that she realized the extent of Burt's fore-
thought. On a saucer beside the tub nestled the pink
fragrance of her own soap, which she had left out
beside the sink next to Burt's clean-smelling house-
hold soap.

Lathering the familiar fragrance over her upper
half, Dani reflected that Burt must be a man of many
faces. Well, she knew that anyway. . . the thoughtful
touch of leaving her soap within easy reach had just
displayed an added aspect of his character as she
knew it. The unbidden thought arose that the woman
who would be the recipient of his love would be
blessed beyond her dreams. In addition to the
physical appeal of his overpoweringly male body,

he apparently possessed a sensitivity rare among men.

But that was something she didn't care to dwell on at the moment. Diligently Dani soaped one leg and raised the other, her toes clinging to the rough wooden edge of the tub as she soaped the length of her leg.

It was then that from one corner of her eye she noticed the smooth movement of a dark blob. Crawling along the rim of the tub, black legs extended, was the most enormous spider she had ever seen.

Her foot slithered down and disappeared beneath the water. Horror bound her thoat to silence as her enlarged eyes watched the progress of the spider. The black body was balanced precariously on the edge of the tub, seemingly hesitant, but then with sudden decision the creature set out on a downward journey toward the pink toes protruding from the soapy water.

"Burt!" she screamed, gathering increased momentum in her lungs for her second *"Burt!"* which came out in a high-pitched scream.

She heard the pound of his feet coming toward the cabin and closed her eyes, vainly hoping to shut out the horrific sight of the spider crawling determinedly downward. The door opened with a crash.

"Dani? What is it?"

She forced her eyes opened and looked once into his face, which was set for an emergency. Shuddering, she pointed a shaky finger at the spider, which had halted its progress halfway down the tub as if sensing danger from the human elements above it.

"T-take it away," she stuttered inanely. "Please, Burt, take it away and kill it."

"For God's sake, it's only a spider!" The deep voice expressed his disgust. Bending across her, he scooped the creature up in his big hand and tramped to the door before dropping it. His eyes were scathing as he came back into the steamy warmth of the cabin. "They're not man-eaters—or woman eaters—around here," he scorned, "whatever they may be like in California."

"I—I have a thing about spiders," she faltered.

"I didn't think you screamed because you were that anxious to have me scrub your back," he agreed, his eyes taking on a different hue as they slanted down over the honeyed skin of her shoulders and lingered on the exposed swell of her breast. "Although now that I'm here. . . ."

Too late Dani hugged her knees to her, saying huskily as color flowed freely up into her cheeks, "That won't be necessary. I—I'm sorry I disturbed you."

He made no effort to leave, instead taking a step or two toward her, a sardonic twist curving his mouth. "You really must be naive if you think you disturbed me more at the woodpile than you are right now."

"Please, Burt. . .leave me alone." Her eyes widened to frightened circles as she watched him drop to a crouching position beside the tub and scoop up a handful of cooling water to let it slide tormentingly down her back.

"Hand me the soap," he ordered, so matter-offactly that Dani lifted it from the saucer and gave it to him.

Only when his work-roughened hand was vigorously rubbing her back did she absorb the incongruity of it all. Here she was sitting in a primitive washtub before a primitive stove, being washed by a primitive man. If it weren't so fright-provoking it would be hilariously funny.

And she *was* afraid, she realized, when her eyes lifted with the intention of giving him a fleeting glance only to find that the hard stare in his eyes caught and held hers. The movement of his hand across her back softened and became a half-conscious sensuous rub, his lids dropping to screen the eyes that looked hungrily at the moist parting of her mouth. Whether her fear was provoked by Burt's intimate closeness or by her own upsurge of undefinable longing, she didn't know...in another moment the question was academic anyway.

She heard the faint moan of protest that came from her own throat even as her lips lifted to accept Burt's kiss. "No...Burt...please."

The battle was over before it really began. As his mouth fastened heavily on hers and his hands lifted her to a standing position, her arms went up instinctively around his strongly set neck and her hands rhythmically stroked the thick short hairs at his nape. The hardened tips of her breasts were crushed to the abrasive thickness of his shirt as Burt gathered her against him, his hands sliding over the slick wetness of her back to her hips as he drew her completely from the bath.

She felt like crushed gossamer in the binding arms that held her. Burt, seeking the breath his rasping lungs demanded, lifted his head only to drop it again at once to nuzzle the soft curve of her throat, the pale rise of her breasts with their pulsingly erect tips.

Deep-throated barks shattered the silence that had been between them, broken only by the occasional drop of burning logs in the grate, and Burt's body tensed against her. When the barks continued unabated, he straightened slowly and turned his head in a listening attitude.

"I'd better go and see what it is," he said with husky thickness, swiveling slowly back to look deep into Dani's eyes, which reflected the same drowsy sensuality as did his. He had already withdrawn from her mentally when he put her from him, his fingers biting into the soft flesh of her shoulders.

Immobile, Dani watched as he went to the door, running his fingers through the disturbed strands of his hair before dropping them to his shirtfront. Dani realized with no sense of shock that her own fingers had opened the thick cotton covering the warm hardness of his chest. The imprint of the short curling hairs must surely be etched on the delicate whiteness of her flesh.

It was a minute or two after Burt had closed the door firmly behind him that strength flowed back into her limbs, allowing her to move and reach for the towel she had placed conveniently near the washtub. The shivers that began to shake her body had nothing to do with the abrasiveness of the worn towel fibers and even less with her nakedness in a room warmed by the potbellied stove.

The madness that had invaded her every nerve ending ebbed quickly and surely after Burt's departure. And it *was* a kind of madness, she told herself as she groped for the clothes she had laid out ready: fresh underwear and white jeans topped by a turquoise-colored sailor-type top. Something about this place made her vulnerable to the male attraction Burt exuded from every pore of his superbly made body. An attraction that many women far more experienced than she in the arts of love would find hard to resist.

But resist she must. A future clouded by the attraction she felt toward a man whose own future held nothing more than a hop and skip before the nearest lawman was something she could well do without. For now, she consoled herself traitorously. Once Marsha had the security of a steady income from Copper Canyon Ranch, Dani's life was her own. If that life included the liaison with a man ostracized from society, so be it. No man had ever affected her emotionally, physically, sensually, the way Burt had. Even if it meant living in a state of what her mother would call sin, Dani knew that her future lay with Burt.

Not now, though. She had business to transact before she told Burt of her decision; the kind of business he would do his best to dissuade her from attempting.

He had already done that, which was why she must make her own way from the cabin to Copper Canyon Ranch. With Randy's help.

ESCAPE FROM THE CABIN had been even easier than she had hoped for. Resting on a fallen log, the panting Randy at her feet, Dani thought wistfully of the desolate cabin Burt would come home to that night.

But maybe he would feel a sense of relief, she reflected, after the previous evening when he had lighted the lamp and seemed strangely subdued as he sat opposite her for the evening meal, a haunch of venison that Dani had looked at askance but devoured with the enjoyment of hunger.

"I'm sorry about what happened earlier," he had said, referring obviously to the scene that had taken place in the cabin after her bath. "It won't happen again."

Stung by his apparent indifference to the traumatic, for her, events of the afternoon, Dani had snapped, "That's one thing you can bet on! The sooner I can shake the dust of this place from my heels the better pleased I'll be." And then her curiosity had got the better of her and she had asked loftily, "Who was it?"

"What?" he had said, obviously bewildered by the question.

"Who was hanging around here this afternoon?"

"Oh." Burt's fingers had clamped down on the bread between his fingers. "No one special, just a hobo looking for a handout."

"And did you give him one?" she had asked dryly.

"Enough meat to carry him through the next day or two," he shrugged.

The indifference he displayed toward her, relieving yet maddening her, had lasted all through the desultory card game they played until she paid her last call to the primitive outhouse perched among the trees. By the time she came back to the cabin, he had stoked the fire and disappeared into his cell-like room. When she awoke in the morning to the joyous spread of the sun's fingers, he had gone.

Now, as she shifted her position on the gnarled surface of the fallen tree, she wondered if she had dreamed the scene that had taken place between them the day before. But no, she couldn't have. Her breasts still tingled from the arousing touch of his fingers, her mouth still felt the bruising pressure of his lips.

I'll come back, Burt, she promised silently, her hand dropping to the dog's silky ears, which he had touched. It didn't matter anymore that he was a fugitive from a law that could never understand his type of man. She would join him in his exile, living and loving in that tumbledown cabin without thought for tomorrow.

She would tell Grant King nothing of what had happened since her taking off from Kamloops. According to Burt, the rancher would have taken it for granted that she would not attempt a visit while the spring runoffs were swelling the creeks and flooding the land around them.

Her eyes dropped to the mud-spattered tips of Burt's boots, inadequately filled by two pairs of his thick socks as well as her narrow feet. They would be hard to explain away, but the man she imagined Grant King to be would hardly aspire to being a connoisseur of women's footwear. In her mind, the man who had stolen Copper Canyon Ranch from her grandfather was a creature devoid of finer sensitivities, immune to the more refined aspects of civilized life. Still, she would have liked to make a more confident appearance than she now presented.

She looked wryly down at the skintight jeans adorning her lower half above the incongruously large brown leather boots, the long-sleeved white T-shirt that hung loosely around her figure. The raincoat she had started out wearing was now cast aside on the tree beside her in deference to the hot sun shining from the brilliant blue of the sky.

With a sudden access of wistfulness, she glanced back at the wooded area behind her. She and Randy couldn't have traversed more than a couple of miles, yet the cabin and Burt already seemed a lifetime away. At first, treading as warily as was possible in the clumsy boots, she had been afraid of coming across Burt as he attended his traps, but as time wore on she knew she would have welcomed seeing his tall broad-shouldered figure, would have felt an overpowering need to throw her arms around him and be similarly embraced by him.

Stupid thoughts, she sighed, rising and picking up her raincoat to sling it across her shoulder. If they met, Burt would try to persuade her again that her fight against Grant King was a useless one, and that was something she could never admit until she had faced the man himself.

With Randy confidently leading the way, she set off again, crossing the small, fast-running creeks where he did, tramping through yet another belt of woodland.

"You sure you know where home is, Randy?" she called after the happily sniffing dog who now showed little signs of his paw injury as he pranced along before her. His only reply was an abstractedly waved tail as his speed increased and he disappeared around a bend in the rough trail. Hastening her clumsy steps, Dani went in pursuit. Randy had been most gentlemanly about waiting for her to catch up until now, but he might disappear altogether when he scented the home ground he hadn't seen in several days.

Bursting from the trees, she teetered to a stop in face of the sights that met her eyes. A lake, wide and spreading, lay not fifty yards from where she stood, trees like the ones she had just come through sweeping down in a rush to its shores. For a minute or two she was caught up in the sheer beauty of the reflected forest in the blue green waters.

Her eyes lifted and turned then, sweeping around to the head of the lake, and her breath stopped in her throat. Even with Randy's yelps of pleasure she would have known that she had found Copper Canyon Ranch at last. A large house, white painted and comfortable looking, hugged the contoured shore and gave substance to the farm buildings ranged around it.

This had been her grandfather's home! Her eyes blurred with tears as they took in the details of neatly arranged corrals and red-sided barns, the small cottages scattered through the trees farther around the lake. How he must have loved it here! No wonder he had never felt the need to venture away from it, even to visit his family in California.

Unable to contain himself any longer, Randy took off at a steady lope in the direction of the buildings, and after a moment Dani followed him. The well-worn trail around the lake was muddier than she had found the terrain so far, and the imprints of many horses' hooves were clearly marked on its surface. But Dani scarcely noticed the heavier going in her awkward boots. A nervous flutter had started up in her stomach as the ranch house drew nearer.

Burt had been right. Grant King wouldn't willingly give up any part of this place, let alone the larger share of it, to virtual strangers, whether or not they were related to Henry Benson.

Her chin came up as she dragged one foot from the clinging mud. Henry Benson—or Hank, as Burt called him—had worked hard on this place for more years than she had lived, and no Johnny-come-lately was going to reap the benefits of that labor.

The open low-roofed building to the left of the house apparently accommodated ranch vehicles—two pickup trucks; a covered, four-wheel-drive jeep; a couple of sleek passenger cars; even a small sports-type car similar to her own except that its blue gray paintwork gleamed from the loving care that had been lavished on it.

Approaching the house along a concrete pathway separating it from neatly kept flower borders and lawns that swept down to the lake's edge, Dani took in the quiet prosperity of the place with its upper-story balcony shading an open lower porch on which comfortable patio furniture had been arranged to take advantage of the lake view.

The white-painted steps leading to the front door echoed hollowly under her feet, emphasizing the general air of quietness about the ranch. Maybe Grant King was out tending to the vast acreage attached to the place, she surmised, but surely such a big house would boast at least a housekeeper. Not a wife. Burt had made that plain.

No bell was visible, so she gave a tentative rap with her knuckles on the smooth white-painted double doors. Nothing happened. Then a more peremptory knock elicited the tapping of impatient heels across an uncarpeted floor, and the door was flung wide.

"Yes?" The young woman who answered the door had spoken automatically, but then her nut-brown eyes went disbelievingly over Dani's disheveled appearance, lingering pointedly on the man-size boots that were obviously much too large for her. "Can I help you?"

"I...I want to see Grant King," Dani said hesitantly, nonplussed by the appearance of a girl not much older than herself, attractively wholesome with her dark brown hair cut to frame the square-jawed face and emphasize the wide set of her brown eyes. A cotton plaid shirt stressed the sleek lines of her slender figure, the matching blue of her jeans clinging tightly to finely outlined hips.

"He isn't here right now," she said coolly. "Maybe I can take a message for him?"

"No," Dani said quickly. "I—I'll wait for him. When do you expect him back?"

The slim shoulders lifted in a shrug. "Who knows with Grant? He's here one minute and gone the next." The brown eyes narrowed in curiosity. "What did you want to see him about"

"A...personal matter. May I come in?" Dani brushed past the other girl without waiting for an answer, her eyes going around the spacious hallway with its air of mellowed maturity, the wide fireplace laid ready with king-size logs, the comfortable-looking chairs set randomly around it, the wide gold carpet following the sweep of shallow stairs to the upper floor. Her grandfather certainly had taste, she congratulated him silently.

"I've told you—" the dark girl stood belligerently before her, barring her way "—Grant may not come back till tomorrow, maybe even the day after. Tell me who you are and what you want and I'll have him get in touch with you."

"Are you his wife?" Dani lifted her eyebrows inquiringly, her eyes going automatically to the girl's slim brown hand, which was ringless.

"Not yet." The small pointed chin lifted aggressively. "But Grant has no secrets from me, so you can tell me what your business is."

"I don't think so." Dani deftly sidestepped the girl and went farther into the hall, noting the several doors that led off it. "I'll wait till he gets back."

With a bravado she was far from feeling, she walked across the hall to the first of the closed doors, opening it and stepping into what was obviously a sitting room with its furniture covered in a mixture of brown leather and cretonne. Behind her she heard the girl's annoyed exclamation, but there was no further effort to detain her. The quick rap of heels on tiled hall told her, as she closed the door, that the girl had gone in search of Grant King.

She didn't care, Dani told herself, if he didn't show up until the next day. She had come a long way by a devious route to have this confrontation with him, and no almost wife was about to deter her.

There was another fireplace in this room, one that stretched the length of one wall and the height of the ceiling. A broad hearth ledge, made of the same light-colored sandstone rocks, invited lounging with its scattered cushions in bright hues along its room-width length. But Dani chose one of the flowered chintz armchairs at right angles to it, and dropped into it with a sense of shock as its soft upholstery enfolded her. She had become so used to Burt's spartan upright chairs that such comfort seemed almost decadent.

Burt! What was he doing now? What would he feel when he got back to the cabin at dusk to find her gone? Probably nothing very much, she reflected sadly. To him she had been nothing more than a convenient female to lighten the days of his self-caused exile. Certainly he could never love her as she... loved him.

The knowledge that she loved Burt came as no violent shock to her senses. It had been there, like the culmination of a dream, since he had carried her from her car. Even here, in these comparatively luxurious surroundings, she could feel the hard touch of his mouth on hers, the expectant swell of her breasts as his rough hands caressed her. Oh, Burt!

Her head lifted as two sets of heels drummed over the tiled hall outside the room where she sat, one heavy, obviously masculine, the other the same light taps of the girl who had admitted her to the house. Her heart leaped erratically in her breast as she straightened in the chair. Fleetingly she wished that she had been able to bathe and change her clothes before facing Grant King. But it was too late now. Already the door was swinging open, and she blinked at the tall figure framed in the doorway. Behind him, the girl who had admitted her was retreating furiously across the hall.

Her eyes focused again on the man silhouetted against the dim light from the hall. Black hair leaped out at her, gleaming black eyes beneath winged eyebrows....

"Burt!" She blinked and shook her head dazedly, knowing, yet not knowing that the man holding himself tautly in the doorway was Burt. "I...I don't understand."

"I can explain, Dani," the deep voice said, and a fury deeper than any she had ever known shook Dani to her core.

Like the pieces of a puzzle, everything dropped into place. No wonder Burt had tried to dissuade her from staking her claim to her grandfather's property! He must have been reporting regularly to Grant King on the disposition of Henry Benson's granddaughter!

"How much did Grant King pay you to put me off coming to the ranch?" she choked, rising from the chair to face him with flashing eyes. The sad, almost shamefaced look about him infuriated her further. "Did he offer you silence about your shady past?"

Burt's jaw clenched to a white line and his long legs covered the distance between them almost before she knew he had moved.

"You don't understand, Dani." His dark eyes seemed to have grown blacker suddenly, and held a tortured kind of sadness she knew must have been born of shame at his deception.

"Oh, I understand all right," she said bitterly, walking from him to stand with her back to the fireless grate, knowing that if she hadn't, the fingers she clenched close to her palms would have raked gougingly across his face. She shook her head in self-mockery. "What an idiot I was not to know that you were defending him for a reason! He's a powerful man, you said, one I couldn't and shouldn't try to fight! Powerful enough to keep the police from nosing too close to your hideout?"

Her voice had risen dangerously, hiding the tears of humiliation she needed to shed, and Burt spoke sharply.

"I didn't defend him for that reason," he said tautly, his skin seeming to have paled under its weatherbeaten tan. "I—"

"What did you do," she jeered, "come over here and report to him every day on how well you were persuading me to forget about our claim to my grandfather's property?"

"I came over here every day, yes," he admitted quietly, "but not to report to him. That would have been hard to do, because—" the look of pain deepened in his eyes "—I *am* Grant King, Dani." He took a step toward her as if to counteract the shock of what he had just said, but Dani's frozen look halted him as she groped for the fireside ledge and half fell onto it.

For a minute or two she thought she was going to faint; the room whirled around her and seemed to break into a thousand jagged pieces. How could Burt be her enemy, Grant King? There was no sense to it, unless....

"I don't believe you," she whispered wanly, lifting her pale face to look unseeingly up at him. "You're just saying that to—"

"It's true, Dani," he broke in gently, stepping forward to grip her elbows with a touch that was almost tender and lift her to her feet. "I didn't want to hurt you—"

He broke off and turned his head with an irritated movement when the door opened and the girl who had let Dani into the house came into the room, stopping just inside the doorway.

"Grant, I'm leav—" Her eyes widened in curious amazement when she took in the intimacy of their stance, then her look changed to one of female venom.

"That's fine, Myra," he said with forced evenness. "I'll see you on Monday."

"Aren't you picking me up for the dance tomorrow night?" she asked frostily, her eyes pointedly ignoring Dani.

"I don't believe so. Jed or one of the other boys will be more than happy to oblige you."

"Thanks for nothing," she snapped brittlely and pivoted on her heel, slamming the door behind her.

Dani had heard the words, but none of them had registered after the first, and all too natural, "Grant." As soon as the other girl had crashed her way out, she pulled herself away from Burt and despised herself for the momentary weakness that had made her lean for support on his hard-muscled body.

But he wasn't Burt anymore. He was Grant King, the man she had come so far to do battle with. An acrid sourness rose in her throat as she sought support instead from the padded back of the chintz-covered armchair flanking the fireplace.

"Look, Dani, you have to let me explain," he began, tautening the close fit of his jeans by pushing his balled fists into his pockets. "My intentions were never—"

"We both know what your intentions were, Mr. King," she cut him off bitterly.

"I don't think you do." His voice overrode the shrill sound of hers, and she glared rebelliously at him. "I want you to marry me, Dani," he said only slightly less harshly.

"You don't say!" she mocked, her fingers tightening on the rough cotton until they grew white. Illogically, she wished that it had been Burt asking her that question, instead of the man who had more to gain than lose by marrying her. "That would settle all your problems nicely, wouldn't it? A bedmate *and* no threat to your boss status. Thanks, but no thanks,

Mr. King," she ended scornfully, "I'll take my chances with the law."

"Dani—"

Ignoring the half warning in his voice, she swept him with her stormy eyes. "So if you'll show me to a vacant bedroom—" she looked expressively around the richly furnished living room "—and I'm sure there must be many in this beautiful home, I'll get settled in. Isn't there a saying somewhere that possession is nine-tenths of the law?" She came out from behind the defensive cover of the chair and faced him boldly. "And I don't doubt you'll be able to use that ingenuity of yours to spirit my things from the hideaway cabin?"

The long line of his jaw contracted momentarily as he looked starkly into her eyes, then he turned away from her, saying curtly, "I'll get Maggie, my housekeeper, to see to the room."

His long stride as he went to the door, and the wide set of his shoulders, sent a physical pain through Dani's middle. He was the man she both loved and hated. The Burt part of him, the part she loved, was so far removed from the arrogant self-seeking of Grant King that they were like two separate entities. It was the Burt part of him she had to forget, the handful of days and nights she had spent with him, learning the depth of her untamed responses to his lovemaking.

CHAPTER SEVEN

THE HOUSEKEEPER, MAGGIE, was a softly plump woman in her middle age, chattering uninhibitedly as she led Dani up the gold-carpeted stairs to the half-galleried floor above.

"I'm sorry I had to keep you waiting while I fixed the room for you," she apologized, clinging breathlessly to the curving wood of the banister as they ascended. "I can't remember the last time Grant had overnight visitors. But he told me to get this room ready for you—" she threw open a door halfway along the left passage off the upper hall "—because it has the nicest view."

It had a nice view, Dani conceded, the wide picture windows encompassing the lake and pine-covered slopes cascading into it. Her grandfather had chosen his site well.

"How long have you been the housekeeper at the ranch?" she questioned suddenly, swinging around to look full into Maggie's face.

"More years than I care to remember," the soft-cheeked woman chuckled, yet her eyes were sharply intelligent as they went over Dani's inelegant outfit.

"Then you must have known my grandfather, Henry Benson?"

"I doubt if there's a person living in the Chilcotin who didn't know Hank Benson," Maggie said comfortably from the door, her eyes growing mistily sentimental. "Who'd have thought that he had a pretty granddaughter like you tucked away somewhere?"

"He never mentioned me?" Dani persisted in her questions, a faintly wistful note in her voice.

"Not that I can recall, honey," the older woman said sympathetically, "but you know what men are like, especially when they get to the age Hank was." She visibly drew herself together before adding, "If there's anything you need, just come and find me in the kitchen. I'll be making supper for seven, as I usually do."

"Thanks...Maggie."

Dani made no move for many minutes after the kindly housekeeper had gone about her business. The hollow at the pit of her stomach spoke painfully of her hunger, unassuaged since that morning's breakfast of porridge. But even if the housekeeper had offered her a meal she doubted if she could have swallowed it. A deathly tiredness seemed to have enveloped her.

Shucking off the boots that had encumbered her for hours, she went to the comfortable-looking double bed with its cotton rose-sprigged comforter and collapsed onto it, wriggling and arching her body until she could pull the thickly puffed quilt over her.

The bed had a heavenly softness she had almost forgotten during her nights on the hard thinness of the cabin mattress, nights when admittedly she had slept deeply and securely. Because Burt had lain in the cell-like room next to hers? Because his voice and hands had been tenderly soothing when his early-morning movements had awakened her?

But Burt didn't exist. There was only Grant King, the man she had vowed to topple from his pinnacle of power....

HER WATCH POINTED to six-thirty when Dani surfaced from sleep and looked dazedly around the unfamiliar room. The polished gleam on heavy, ornately scrolled furniture caught the added glow of a fast-setting sun, and instead of the spartan, almost primitive surroundings she had expected there was the solid respectability of tastefully blended furniture with a gold and white complementary color scheme in broadloom and wallpaper.

A hunger that was now gnawing insistently at her innards provided the impetus for her throwing back of the quilt and the propulsion of her feet to the thickly carpeted floor. She had never been so hungry in all of her life.

She staggered to the foot of the bed and looked blankly at the luggage holder in which her own suitcase lay in solitary state. Burt—Grant—must have brought it there. Her fumbling fingers at last managed to open the snap locks, and unaccountable tears filled her eyes when she saw her hairbrush tucked in neatly next to her toilet bag. Oh, Burt, Burt!

The tantalizing aroma of food cooking permeated her dulled senses, and she was made agonizingly aware again of the emptiness of her stomach.

Unpacking only her toilet things and a short hyacinth blue nylon robe, she went in search of a bathroom, pausing at the door to come back to the suitcase and rummage thoughtfully through it. She needed to wear something tonight that would give her confidence to face the man who was probably even now waiting down below. After more than a week of being packed in a suitcase her clothes seemed to have been permanently pressed into new lines, but the black silk jersey she at last selected would lose its creases in the bathroom steam.

The passage was empty and quiet when she went tentatively from her room, and she was relieved to find that the first door she opened led to the biggest bathroom she had ever seen. Closing and locking the door firmly behind her in case this was the bathroom used by Grant King, too, she glanced around the spacious room, guessing from its size and quality modern fixtures that it had been converted from a small bedroom. A marbleized vanity and sink unit along one wall housed cupboards and drawers beneath and full-width mirrors above. A man-size tub it must be Grant King's bathroom— drew her eyes because of the shower head fixed above it.

She had forgotten the luxury of standing under a warm cleansing spray with an unlimited supply of hot water. At least, she thought hastily, reaching for the shampoo bottle, she hoped the supply was unlimited. Her hands stopped in midmotion as she lathered her hair. No wonder Burt had always seemed as if he bathed reasonably often! While she had been making do with cat-lick washes, he had had access to un-limited baths and showers here at the house.

Fury was still tightly compressing her lips twenty minutes later when she stood ready to descend to the floor below. The makeup she had mainly dispensed with at the cabin was now subtly blended on her skin to give her face a less innocent look, and the black dress, clinging to the curves of her figure, lent an added sophistication. She had debated, after drying her hair with her small travel dryer, whether she should arrange it more severely, but time didn't permit so it hung in silky falls to her shoulders, turning up slightly there. She was ready to do battle with Grant King.

The murmur of voices came from the sitting room in which she had spent the traumatic half hour earlier, and she paused at the open door, listening unashamedly to what was obviously the tail end of a serious conversation.

"Just play it by ear, Maggie, I don't know what else to do at this point." Grant's voice, as he spoke to the housekeeper, sounded frustrated and tired somehow. "She's hell-bent on doing what she came here for."

Maggie sounded far less strained and even jocular when she said, "I've never known you beaten yet, especially by a woman."

"This one's different, Maggie, she—" He looked up when Dani pushed open the door to its fullest extent, and she was rewarded by the stunned look in his eyes for the care she had taken over her appearance.

"I'm sorry if I'm late," she said coolly to the

housekeeper, who had a similarly shocked look about her. Giving both pairs of shocked eyes the full benefit of her modeling experience, she crossed to stand next to Grant in front of the fireplace. "It took quite a while to clean off the effects of conditions I've lived under for the past few days."

"Oh, yes." Maggie slanted an embarrassed sideways look at Grant, then forced a smile to her face. "There's no hurry—supper can wait awhile until you've had a drink to relax you." She bustled out of the room after another nervous look in Grant's direction.

He cleared his throat. "Would you like to have a drink?"

While he listed what was available, Dani thought furiously. The last thing she needed on an empty stomach was the potent effect of alcohol on her system; on the other hand, to maintain the cool role of sophisticated woman, it would help to turn a glass stem in her fingers.

"I'll have vermouth on the rocks," she interrupted his recital, hiding her surprise at the extent of his bar in the unsophisticated world he lived in.

But he seemed to have divined her thoughts, saying over his shoulder as he went to the dark maple buffet along the far wall, "Strange as it may seem to you, we do quite a lot of entertaining here, especially around Christmas."

As he busied himself among the glasses and bottles, Dani studied his broad back and flat hips, intimately familiar yet unfamiliar in the white sweater and dark blue worsted slacks. Even more unusual, she noted as he came back with the two glasses, was the silky white shirt and blue-striped tie visible under the V neck of the sweater. *What the well-dressed rancher wears in his leisure hours,* she mocked silently.

She took the chair he indicated before reaching up for the glass he held out to her, the inevitable contact of their fingers sending an icy shiver over her.

"You must have missed that." She nodded sourly at the stubby glass of whiskey over ice in his other hand. "Or did you drink your fill here before coming back to the cabin at night?"

The sadness she had noticed earlier lurking deep down in his eyes seemed to intensify momentarily. "I enjoy a drink after the day's work is through, but it's something I can take or leave alone." He moved away but didn't sit down, resuming instead his previous stance before the empty fireplace. A flicker of the familiar gleam danced across his eyes as he looked down at her. "You'd have known if I'd been drinking, wouldn't you?" he asked softly.

Dani's eyes dropped to the drink in her hand, and she lifted it quickly to take a sip too large. Fighting against the humiliation of choking, she felt the warmth flowing down through her, its effect instantaneous on her empty stomach.

When her breathing had returned to normal, she looked up at him scornfully. "I suppose making love to me was part of your plan to get me to forget Copper Canyon Ranch existed? What were you going to do, suggest I go back home and wait till the police weren't interested in you anymore?"

"I didn't tell you I was hiding out from the police."

"No, but you let me go on assuming you were a thief, an outlaw," she shot back, forgetting the control she had been determined to maintain in her dealings with him.

As it was, he was the one to keep cool and collected. His black lashes were clearly marked against his cheeks as he looked down into the glass he swirled gently in his hand. "I asked you to marry me," he pointed out quietly.

"Certainly you did," she scorned, "after I'd found out the game you were playing. Did you expect me to trip over my feet in my hurry to accept?"

"I thought you might consider it. The lovemaking wasn't entirely on my part, was it?"

Dani took another gulp of the vermouth, playing for time to seek an answer, though her head was already affected by the alcohol.

"You took advantage of the circumstances," she said huskily at last.

"You might recall which one of us called the shots as far as control went," he pointed out dryly, knowing his point had gone home from the sudden rise of color in her cheeks. "Does that sound to you as if I was trying to take advantage? Believe me, if I'd wanted to do that, nothing would have been easier."

The door opened with a noisy rattle of the handle and Maggie saved Dani's reply by telling them that their soup was on the table.

Downing the last of her drink in an effort to still the jumpy nerves in her stomach, Dani rose and went to the door, closely followed by Grant, who had done the same with his glass.

The dining room he led her into down the hall was a spacious but homely room with a long ranch-style table stretched down its center, another fireplace adorning one wall and various buffets and servers in dark maple ranged around the rest of the room. To the left, full-length gold velvet curtains sweepingly covered the window area. Two places had been laid at one end of the long table, and Grant held her chair so that she had no option but to take the inferior side seating while he settled himself at the head of the table as to the manner born.

Dani cast a scathing glance down the table at all the empty places. "Don't you feel just a little ridiculous sitting here by yourself all the time?"

"Not all the time," he corrected, picking up his spoon to tackle the appetizing soup, thick with colorful vegetables and dark meat, before him. "As I told you, I entertain quite a lot. And—" his mouth quirked at the corners in a way she remembered "—I intend to fill up quite a few of those empty places when I marry." Plying his spoon, he savored a mouthful of soup before saying casually, "How do you feel about children? Do you want a big family?"

"Nothing like the size it would take to fill this table," she threw back tartly before giving in to the overwhelming desirability of the soup. Much, much later, when her plate was almost empty, she took in the import of his words. Had he been proposing again, in a roundabout way? "Anyway, it's none of your business whether I have one or twenty children."

"It certainly is," he retorted unheatedly. "I have to admit I'd been thinking along the lines of five or six maximum. But if you want to go for more. . . ." He shrugged.

"What I'm trying to tell you, Mr. King," she grated through clenched teeth, "is that the size of my family has nothing to do with the size of yours." She sat back in her chair and waved a dismissing hand. "I have no intention of marrying you, now or ever."

"You mean all those children—" his eyes went from place to place around the table as if counting innumerable black heads and dark eyes "—are going to be born of unwed parents? How can you do that to your own children?"

"They won't *be* my children," she gritted, her blue eyes sparking fury at him as Maggie came into the room bearing a substantial tray.

As the well-rounded housekeeper unloaded dishes containing colorful and succulent vegetables and ribs braised in a bubbling red sauce, her eyes went anxiously from one diner to the other, lingering on Dani's mutinously set face.

"It's a long time since anyone as pretty as you sat at this table," she said sentimentally, then frowned. "In fact, I don't remember anyone as—"

"I'm not open to flattery, Mrs.—Maggie," Dani damped down the older woman's enthusiasm. But she felt no sense of triumph when the plump cheeks trembled and the pale blue eyes looked to Grant King as if for support.

"Thanks, Maggie," he said gently, "everything looks great."

Dani knew that she had been witchy and bitchy as the downcast housekeeper hurried from the room, but the tears rising suddenly to the back of her eyes had no release when she remembered that Maggie was a willing participant in Grant King's fraudulent schemes. They must both think she was completely idiotic to believe that she would be captivated by Grant's talk of marriage and children.

He, however, seemed to have different views about Maggie as he handed Dani in turn the glazed carrots, creamy mashed potatoes and buttered turnips.

"Did you have to upset Maggie like that?" his thinly drawn lips opened to say at last. "I hadn't thought of you as being cruel."

Stung, Dani tossed her hair back and looked directly into his eyes. "Then you'd better start thinking that way, Mr. King," she said hardly. "I have no intention of marrying you, or," she stressed, "keeping on as housekeeper a woman who obviously has no more ethical sense than you have."

"You don't know what you're talking about!" he shot back harshly, piling food onto his plate as if he wasn't aware of his actions.

"Did you stock up on food, too, every time you came over here?" she mocked, derisive eyes on his laden plate. "While I lived on porridge and whatever revolting creatures you managed to catch or trap?"

The tension seemed to go out of him suddenly as he picked up his fork. "I ate the same as you," he said quietly. Then, with the air of a man hungry for food, he fell silent as he started on his meal.

Dani watched him for a further minute, then, shrugging, picked up her own fork. The ribs, complemented by a tangy sauce, were delicious, as were the crisply cooked vegetables, and she felt no desire to talk as she assuaged the hunger that had been building in her for days. She pushed away the thought that Grant, if he was telling the truth, must have a proportionately larger appetite to satisfy.

Maggie's full lips were pursed into what Dani guessed to be an unusually firm line as she served Baked Alaska for dessert and left a heavy silver coffee tray for them to help themselves. Dani tried to break the disapproving aura surrounding the housekeeper by congratulating her on a delicious meal, but Maggie barely acknowledged the olive branch.

"I'm glad it was to your liking." Her brows lifted as she looked at Grant. "If there's nothing else you need, I'll put the dishes on to wash and get on home."

Dani's head lifted in surprise. She had assumed that Maggie lived at the ranch house, but it seemed not. The momentary panic that washed over her was stemmed instantly. She had spent several nights alone with Burt—Grant—in the isolated cabin, so there was little to fear from sharing this big house with him.

"That's fine, Maggie. See you tomorrow."

The housekeeper's good-night was a general one, but Dani had a feeling it applied only grudgingly to herself. So what, she queried silently as Maggie made her way to the door with the empty plates. She was in on Grant King's devious schemes and deserved none of the kindness Dani would normally have given her gladly.

"I'd like to call my mother," she said abruptly into the silence that fell after Maggie's departure, adding with a sarcastic slant to her mouth, "or are the phone lines still down?" A stab of irritation, or pain, went through her when Grant looked at her, and she knew instantly that the telephone never had been out of order. "You'll never know how much I despise you," she hissed in a low, furious tone. "Fooling me is one thing, but leaving my mother to worry about me unnecessarily is something else again. Where's your phone?"

"In the hall, but—"

Dani was off her chair and running before he had time to say more. She found the cream-colored telephone on a table under the arch of the stairs and, going through a laconic operator, heard her home phone ringing regularly in her ear.

"Mom?" she said eagerly when the receiver was picked up. "It's me, Dani."

"Oh, hi, honey," the dearly familiar voice said with less concern—a lot less concern—than Dani had expected.

"I'm sorry I haven't been able to contact you before this," she apologized hurriedly, "but I've been—"

"No need to worry, honey," her mother's voice came comfortably over the wire, "Grant explained everything when he called."

"Grant?" Dani stared blankly at the curving wood of the staircase. "He called you?"

"Of course, darling. We talked for quite a while, and he explained that you couldn't call yourself because you were out looking over the property. Tell me—" her mother's voice lightened to faintly gurgling laughter "—is the place so big that it takes days to look it over?"

"Yes, it's big, mom," Dani said automatically while she tried to gather her scattered wits. Why hadn't he told her he had called her mother? He had known how worried she was.

"Does he look as nice as he sounds, Dani?" her mother's voice came again, gently quizzing.

"He looks like dad in a temper, except that he's darker," Dani said with unusual viciousness, and heard her mother's startled exclamation.

"Isn't that strange! When he called me, he reminded me of your father somehow."

"There's no real resemblance," Dani said shortly, aware suddenly that Grant had come to the door of the dining room and was listening openly to her conversation. Remembering belatedly that she had no intention of upsetting Marsha, which a recital of her recent ordeal would certainly do, she said lightly, "Dad was a lot more refined in his nature than Grant King. . . . Yes, I guess he's more like grandfather than dad. . . . No, don't go yet, mom. . . ." She turned her back on Grant's implacably placed figure and blinked hard against the sudden tears that threatened her eyes. "What?. . . No, I'm okay. . . . I don't now, but I'll call you again soon. . . ."

She stood with her hand on the receiver long after the conversation was over, fighting for the control she knew she needed to face Grant King. More than ever, she knew after speaking to the gentle Marsha, she had to fight for the inheritance that was theirs, for the treatments Marsha needed for her well-being. It helped that a slow fury was beginning to build in her because of her mother's evident gullibility where Grant was concerned, and the fact that he had taken full advantage of Marsha's trusting nature. He was good at taking advantage of unsuspecting females.

The tears she blinked back at that moment were due more to the frustration she felt at her own stupidity than to any sense of loss her emotions were undergoing because she had actually thought herself in love with him. Love might be blind, she told herself bleakly as she retraced her steps across the hall, but her eyes would be totally clear when she fought Grant King for the ranch.

CHAPTER EIGHT

SURPRISINGLY, SHE SLEPT WELL although it was early when she woke and blinked unknowingly around the unfamiliar room, which was illuminated only dimly by the dawn light filtering through the finely meshed curtains.

She lay inert in the comfortable bed, warmly enclosed within thick blankets and high-raised comforter. The house was still with the hush of early morning, and she made no attempt to rise.

Which of these bedrooms on the upper floor had been her grandfather's? The one in which Grant King now slept? Her mouth curved in a bitter arc. He would have had little compunction about taking over his benefactor's room in the same way as he had usurped the rest of the property.

That thought reminded her of her parting shot the evening before when she had wrested herself from the confining grip of his arms.

"I'll be inspecting the property tomorrow," she had told him, her pale cheeks warmed by the fury that filled her.

"All of it?" he had asked with an arrogant lift of his brows.

"Every inch of it!"

"That could take some time, unless you're a skilled horsewoman?"

His evident amusement had flicked her on the raw, and at the same time made her falter in the face of his confidence.

"I meant," she bit off sharply, "the house and buildings, of course."

"Of course," he had agreed as if humoring a willful child, a quirk still at the corners of his mouth as he added, "If you'll tell me what time you'll be ready, I'll give you an escorted tour."

"I can manage myself." A vision of savage bulls and untrained horses had flashed across her mind, and she amended, "I mean, the house. You can take me around outside."

"I'll look forward to it."

His look of irony had been the one she carried from the room, but now her memory went reluctantly back to the scene before that, the one in which he had jerked her from the sitting-room chair she occupied and into his arms, his calm deserting him as his eyes blazed down into hers. What had she said to make him so angry? Something about hating him and her intention of making him an offer for his share of the ranch that he wouldn't be able to refuse.

"There's only one thing you could offer me that I wouldn't be able to refuse," he had gritted, his fingers gouging into the soft flesh of her arms.

"And that's something I'm not likely to offer you on a plate," she said vindictively, vainly trying to free herself from his grip, but feeling a surprising lack of fear when she couldn't.

"You've done that several times." His cutting tone had sliced into Dani's brain. It was true, she would have surrendered to the overwhelming passion Burt had the power to stir in her.

"I...didn't know who you were then," she said tautly, her nostrils flaring as she glared defiantly up at him.

"I'm the same man," he pointed out, with what must seem to him like irrefutable logic. But logic was far from Dani's mind, her heart.

"You're not," she had choked. "You're a cheat, and a liar—you even thought up a false name out of the blue."

"It wasn't out of the blue," he said dismissingly. "My middle name is Wilburt, and my grandmother always called me that because it was her husband's name." His eyes narrowed on hers. "Anyway, you thought I was a thief hiding out from the world, but that didn't stop you. What's so different now?"

A dozen different reasons had rushed to her mind, but she had been incapable of articulating them. The awareness of his work-toughened hands on her soft flesh, the electric feel of his hard body pressed to hers, had hit her like a bolt of lightning and left her knees threatening collapse.

"Mmm?" It was as if he had sensed her weakening and used that husky mumble to complete her downfall. However it happened, her mouth had no need of his fingers under her chin to raise its parted breathlessness to the inevitable descent of his, the inevitable scratch of his beginning stubble, the inevitable. . . .

It was then that she had twisted out of his arms,

despising her own weakness, hating the advantage he had taken of it.

Because Grant King was an entirely different person from the Burt she had come to love in a few short days. Grant had something to gain—a lot to gain—from a love relationship with her. Mainly a wife who would keep the wealth in the family. Burt had wanted nothing more from her than the fulfillment of his natural desire for a woman to share his life, for however short a time.

Dani's head twisted on the pillow as the sound of a running shower came from the bathroom next door. Grant was up and preparing to face his day. The buzz of an electric razor minutes later set her thoughts off in another direction.

At the cabin he had shaved without benefit of modern accoutrements. Yet his razor had been there, as well as the soap and towels they had both used. What was he doing in a tumbledown shack when he had all the luxuries he could ever need right here at the ranch house? Come to that, what had he been doing living there at the time her car had crashed, the stubble of days adding to the wild recluse appearance that had initially given her the idea that he was a fugitive from the law?

Those questions worried her until, after a kitchen breakfast served by a remote Maggie, she set off with Grant on a tour of the ranch building.

Crossing the side lawn beside the house, Dani glanced up into Grant's closed-off expression that left the questions trembling on her lips. He looked so different from the Burt she had come to know so well in the space of a few days that he was unapproachable. The stone-colored shirt and pants were similar to the work clothes he had worn at the cabin, but it was as if he had removed himself from her mentally this morning.

She scarcely noticed the neatly fenced corrals they skirted, the barns smelling sweetly of seasoned hay, the stockyards where plump hens pecked busily at the hardened mud. It was only when they came to a paddock fenced with wire and wood supports that Grant lost some of his cool politeness and allowed enthusiasm to creep into his voice as he pointed out a mare and foal in the distance.

"That's Cassandra and her colt, Benny."

"Benny?" Dani questioned, amazed at the speed with which mother and son covered the ground to reach Grant's familiar figure.

Grant gave her a sideways look, his mouth lifting in a sardonic line. "Named after your grandfather."

"Oh, Benny...Benson. I see," she said thoughtfully as the pair cantered up to the fence, ignoring her while their graceful necks stretched up to receive Grant's rough caress. She would have liked to touch the smooth coats herself, especially the dark chestnut of her grandfather's namesake, but horses were an unknown element to her. The teeth Cassandra bared in pleasure at Grant's touch could sink deep into her own flesh, and she shuddered at the thought.

Sensing her discomfort, Grant put his hand under her elbow and led her away from the yearning horses. "Have you never ridden?" he asked casually as they

veered away from the neatly laid-out bungalows
nestled along the lakeshore.

"L.A. isn't exactly a horseman's paradise," she
quipped lightly, hoping he wouldn't take his warmly
encompassing hand from her elbow, and feeling a
sense of letdown when he did.

"I suppose not. It must be hard for somebody
raised in the city to feel at home in a place like this."

His steps had turned in the direction of a high red
barn situated close to the paddock enclosing the
horses, and Dani automatically followed him into its
lofty coolness. The sweet scent of hay filled her
nostrils with a primitive satisfaction that must be a
throwback to her grandfather's love of this wilderness country. It was strange: she could find no trace
of her grandfather's spirit in the graciously beautiful
house, but here at the core of the ranch he seemed to
become a living entity.

She swung around with luminously misty eyes to
say something like that to Grant, but the words faded
and died when she saw that he had been observing
her with a deep, brooding look that seemed, in the
dim light, to hold a measure of calculation.

"Dani," he said huskily, lifting his arms as if to
pull her to him, but she sidestepped him quickly and
walked to the wide-open barn doors.

"Thanks for the tour," she said crisply. "I can
look around the house on my own."

She put distance between them, too much for her
to have heard anything he said, if indeed he said
anything. A strange emotion caught and swelled in
her throat as she made her way back to the com-

fortably situated house. Henry Benson had walked in this direction many times, maybe even in the traces of her own footprints, but she wished confusedly that her grandfather had never set foot on it. And then she would never have met Grant King, never have known what it was to love a man who could never be more than a myth to her.

THE GROUND FLOOR of the house yielded no more than a hasty glimpse into a world that spoke more of Grant King than the aged grandfather she imagined. Starting in the kitchen, where an active Maggie brooked no refusal of the coffee she set on the square gingham-covered table, it was Grant, not her grandfather, who was uppermost in her mind.

"Is Grant coming in for coffee?" the housekeeper demanded almost belligerently when Dani seated herself at the table, feeling it was more trouble to refuse than accept the proferred drink.

"I...I don't know. He was in one of the barns when I left him."

"Hmph! He must be looking at the new little mare. We've almost lost her two or three times over the past few days." To Dani's uncomprehending look she explained brusquely, "Dandy—she had a hard time birthing the little one, and it's only thanks to Grant that she delivered safely."

The role of midwife wasn't one Dani would have assigned to Grant King, but according to Maggie he was the best veterinarian God had seen fit to create.

"He's a good man," she said belligerently, her pale blue eyes daring Dani to contradict her. "Ask anyone around here, they'll tell you the same as I'm telling you now.''

As Dani made her escape to the rest of the house she reflected wryly that no one but Maggie was available to elicit a character reference from. Not that it mattered. She had already made up her mind about Grant King.

The compact office across the hall from the sitting room contained a sizable desk, and ranch account books ranged on shelves along one wall. The dark green covers held little interest for her, she decided, flicking the neatly inscribed pages through her fingers. She knew instinctively that her grandfather would have left the accounting work in Grant's hands. A typing desk, replete with typewriter, stood in juxtaposition to the managerial desk. It was small wonder that Myra, working in such close proximity to a bachelor boss, fostered dreams of becoming Mrs. Grant King. As far as she was concerned, Grant would be an enviable catch in the marriage stakes. Young, handsome, well set up financially. Any woman's dream.

Her hand hesitated only fractionally on the door of Grant's bedroom on the upper floor. None of the other rooms there had given evidence, on a cursory inspection, of having housed Henry Benson until his death a few months earlier. And why would they, Dani questioned, pushing the door to Grant's room fully open. This was the space her grandfather had occupied while he built up the ranch to its present prosperity.

Pushing aside her guilt feelings at invading Grant

King's privacy, she opened drawers and cupboards in the male, spartan room, seeking evidence of her grandfather's existence. A sense of futility filled her when her questing hands turned up only neatly arranged underwear and folded sweaters. Every trace of Henry Benson had been systematically eliminated.

Her eye fell on the night table beside the king-size bed, and shrugging, she crossed to it and slid open the narrow drawer under it. Her mouth fell open when she looked down at the only article it contained: a glossy publicity picture of herself.

She sat shakily on the edge of the bed, not removing the picture from the drawer. It must be the one Marsha had sent to her grandfather over a year before. Which proved, she told herself, that this had been his room. A lump formed in her throat. He had kept close to his bed this one memento of a granddaughter he had never seen in person.

Minutes later, another thought occurred to her. Grant King must have seen this photograph, must have known who she was when he first laid eyes on her! She caught her lip between her teeth at the memory of how quickly he had formed his plan to keep her away from Copper Canyon Ranch. He was clever, no doubt about that. But—she brushed a hand across her eyes and jumped to her feet—he was about to find out that she wasn't the sweet innocent she looked in that picture! Besides putting in her claim to the larger part of the ranch, she would sue him for abducting her and keeping her at the cabin against her will. Snatching up the picture, she went in search of him.

As IT HAPPENED, the search was short. Running down the gold-carpeted stairs, she heard the murmur of voices from the kitchen. Caution quieted her feet as she crossed the hall and approached the door, which was slightly ajar.

"...tell you, it upsets me, Grant," Maggie was saying, the chink of dishes indicating that she was fixing lunch. "You heard how she spoke to me last night, and I don't like it."

Grant's reply was dry. "It's not exactly the easiest situation in the world for me, either. But if it bothers you, take the rest of the weekend off as usual. By Monday I'll have things worked out the way I want them to be. She'll marry me, Maggie, if I have to—"

"If you have to what?" Dani asked coolly, walking into the room and feeling a flash of triumph as both faces swung on her in startled guilt. "Abduct me again?"

Grant, throwing down the towel he had been using by the sink, found his voice first. "What do you...." His eyes went down to the picture she held in her hand, narrowing as he quickly lifted them to her face again. "Where did you get that?" he demanded harshly.

"Where my grandfather put it, in a drawer beside his bed!" she flashed back angrily. "You didn't get around to moving that with the rest of his stuff, did you?"

"You've got it all wrong, honey," a distraught Maggie put in. "Your grandfather never—"

"I'll see to this, Maggie," Grant interrupted brusquely.

"In the same way you're going to see that I marry you?" Dani taunted, pink color high in her cheeks. "You're not *that* powerful, Mr. Grant King! I wouldn't marry you even if I liked you—which I don't!"

Maggie made a disgusted gesture with her hands and looked up determinedly into Grant's steely-jawed face. "She has to be told, Grant, it's not fair that she has to go on thinking that—" She interrupted herself to look with sympathetic eyes at Dani. "Come and sit down, honey, I think you'll need a seat under you when I tell you what you have to be told."

"I'm all right where I am," Dani said crisply, but there was a faint flicker of uncertainty in the look she sent to Grant's immobile face. "Go ahead and tell me what I need to know." Her tone made it more than clear that nothing Maggie could say would deter her from her purpose.

"You couldn't have found that picture beside your grandfather's bed, honey," Maggie said gently, "because he never spent one night in this house."

Dani stared blankly into her kindly eyes. "What?" she asked faintly.

Maggie shook her head. "He didn't own any part of Copper Canyon Ranch, either. Grant here bought it outright from the old people who used to own it."

Grant moved at last and caught her as she paled and took a staggering step toward the chair she had spurned moments before.

"Let me go." She pushed feebly against the muscled arms holding her and found herself deposited in the chair, her elbows supporting her head on clenched fists. Then anger seeped through her trembling limbs and she looked defiantly into Maggie's face. "You're lying," she said bluntly. "My grandfather wrote and told us about his ranch—this ranch. He wouldn't have lied to us."

"He didn't mean to lie," Grant said quietly from above her head. "He just wanted to have his family feel proud of him. Life hadn't been easy for Hank, and he felt he'd let your father down by not being there to bring him up. He wanted his granddaughter to be proud of him, so he fantasized a little."

Dani drew a deep breath. "A little!"

"All right, a lot." His hand dropped to Dani's shoulder and moved there in soothing rhythm, his voice soft as he said huskily, "You won't hear me say anything against old Hank, though. He brought you here, and that's something I'll always be grateful to him for."

"Don't patronize me anymore!" Dani threw off his hand as she pushed back the chair and got drunkenly to her feet. Hatred like molten lead was flowing through her. She hated her grandfather for his deception, hated the humiliation he had subjected her to, and she hated Grant King for.... With an animal like cry of distress she turned and ran from the kitchen, from Grant's eyes that held the same sadness she had seen several times, from Maggie's anxiously creased expression.

STILL PACING HER BEDROOM FLOOR like a caged leopard an hour later, Dani knew that she had to get away from Copper Canyon Ranch, from Grant, from Maggie. . . .

Waves of humiliation continued to wash over her as the thoughts went around in tightly woven circles in her head. Again and again she heard her own peremptory voice telling Grant that she would make an inspection of the house and farm buildings. How he must have been secretly laughing at her! But no, what he had actually been doing was much worse. He had felt sorry for her, so sorry that he had kept up his pretense of wanting to marry her.

And the marriage bit had come only after she had found her own way to the ranch. Before that, Burt, as she still thought of the cabin man, had been willing to have her stay with him, live with him without benefit of marriage. Until she grew tired of pursuing the hopeless cause of her inheritance? Oh, he had been attracted to her, in the physical way of men who chose other women for their wives, like the Myra who had first admitted her to the ranch. There had obviously been something between the two of them for the girl to tell Dani that she wasn't yet Mrs. Grant King.

Thank God she hadn't told him about her mother's need for expensive treatments! That would have increased his sense of obligation to marry and provide for poor old Hank Benson's destitute family.

She had to get away, but how? Her car was still stuck in that. . . . She stopped pacing and widened her eyes. Could it be that the car she had seen parked safely, and gleaming, in the vehicle shed was her car? The more she thought of it, the more she was convinced that the blue gray vehicle was her own. From the trim state of the other machinery around the ranch, she guessed that Grant's meticulous nature would force him to haul her car from the ditch and have it cleaned and serviced. But where would he have put the keys?

Almost before the thought had formed she was on her way downstairs, pulling up short when Maggie, en route to the kitchen from the dining room, looked up and saw her.

"Would you like some lunch now?" she asked with a tentative smile that smote Dani's conscience with the memory of her own rudeness the night before.

"No, I—I'm not hungry, thanks." She hesitated before getting out, "Maggie, I—thank you for telling me. About. . . . Before I made a bigger fool of myself than I had already."

"Nobody thought you were a fool, honey," the housekeeper said softly. "I've never seen Grant so upset, and I've known him ever since he came to the Canyon."

Dani looked apprehensively around the hall. "Is he—is he around?"

"No, he had a call that one of the steers had got out on the road, so he went to fix that. He shouldn't be long, though," Maggie added with a faintly knowing gleam in her eye. "He'll be glad to know that you're feeling better now. He gives the impression of being hard at times, but underneath he's the kindest man you'd ever wish to meet."

So kind that he would go to the length of marrying a girl he felt sorry for? Dani hid the sourness of that unspoken thought and said casually, "I thought I'd take a walk around the place—I didn't see it all this morning."

"Good," Maggie beamed, turning away. "I'll leave some cold chicken and salad in the fridge in case you feel hungry after your walk. Oh—" she halted and looked back over her shoulder "—and there's a casserole stew doing slowly in the oven for your supper. It doesn't matter how late you have it."

"Thanks, Maggie," Dani said with an awkwardness born of guilt at deceiving the housekeeper. With any luck, she would be far away from the ranch by supper time. She felt a strong twinge of regret that she wouldn't see the kindly Maggie anymore after that brief encounter in the hall.

But regrets were pushed far to the back of her mind minutes later when she inspected the vehicle shed and found that her suspicion was correct. The spic-and-span sports model was hers, and furthermore, the keys dangled idly in the ignition.

She waited until she saw Maggie's plump figure cut across the lawn in the direction of the neatly laid-out houses along the lakeshore, and then she moved quickly, hoping that Grant's business would keep him occupied until she was well away from Copper Canyon Ranch.

Up in her room again, she looked down at her close-fitting jeans and pale blue shirt and decided to change into the suit she had worn for her arrival in the Chilcotin country. It would be more suitable for checking into a motel in Kamloops, which she would have to do now because of the lateness of the afternoon.

Ignoring the hunger pangs brought about by a fleeting vision of the cold chicken and salad Maggie had mentioned, she repacked the clothes she had hung up only the night before in the spacious closet, and threw in her hairbrush and toilet bag before snapping the locks on her suitcase. The journey downstairs and out to the car was accomplished without trouble, but she hoisted her case into the trunk with a softly drawn breath of regret.

Her eyes went around the visible parts of the ranch, the comfortable old house, the neatly fenced corrals, the red-painted barns, the pine-fringed lake that glittered under the afternoon sun. As she had said once to Burt, Marsha would have loved it here.

Thoughts of her mother occupied her mind as she started the engine and backed quietly from the parking space. Marsha would never see the wild beauty of this country, or the ranch she believed had belonged to Henry Benson. And she would never have the treatment she needed to make life more comfortable, not on the salary Dani would make as a receptionist in an office somewhere in L.A.

She turned off the ranch driveway onto the road that must be the one she had been traveling when the car had slithered down into the ditch. The two bridges she crossed in rapid succession showed signs of recent repair, and she reflected bitterly that Grant hadn't lied about that, at least. The creeks that the bridges had spanned were running full and fast still, although the meadows at either side of the narrow road were considerably drier than they had been a week earlier.

Her fingers tightened on the wheel. Was it possible that so much could have happened in such a short time? That the dreams of money to provide comfort for Marsha had been shattered into a million pieces, that she herself had fallen in love with a man who had no basis in reality?

Oh, Burt, Burt... why couldn't you have been what you said you were? A fugitive from justice whom she could love freely, uninhibitedly. Not Grant King, who had power enough to show compassion to a girl who had been deluded by her grandfather.

Her hand lifted to brush the tears from her eyes, but her vision was still blurred when she returned her hand to the wheel. An hallucinatory figure... no, *two* figures... materialized on the road ahead. A horse... Josh... and a man... Burt. Her foot jammed down on the accelerator. She couldn't give in to the tricks her mind was playing on her, or she would spend the rest of her life fighting off the phantoms of what might have been.

The figures stayed put as she rushed toward them, although the horse lifted his head and shook it as if in fright. Too late almost Dani knew that the figures were real, and that she was on the point of slamming into them, of— Her foot lifted from the accelerator and stamped automatically on the brake pedal while her frozen hands jerked the wheel sideways. The car skittered along the thicker gravel at the roadside before its speed was finally, and joltingly, brought to a shuddering halt with its nose pointed down into the ditch.

This time she wasn't hurt, but she was too weak to do anything about the big tears that welled up in her eyes and rolled down her cheeks. She looked helplessly up at Grant when he opened the door and bent to glare in at her, white-faced.

"What in the name of all that's holy do you think you're doing?" he asked explosively, half dragging her from the seat and putting one arm around her when she sagged at the knees and half fell on him. "Am I fated to spend the rest of my life hauling you out of ditches?"

"I—I—oh, Burt, I nearly killed you!" her voice came out in a whisper, her hands going falteringly around his waist to cling tightly to his shirt at the back.

"Well, you didn't," he growled, although there was tenderness in the feel of his arms as they encompassed her and drew her to the strong shelter of his body. "Although whether I'll be able to say that fifty years from now is anybody's guess!"

"F-fifty years?"

"After I've been married to you for that length of time," his voice rumbled against her ear, which, she realized suddenly, was lying flat against his wide chest. She should pull away from it, she knew, but her brain was too shocked to issue the necessary instruction to her body.

"I'll never marry a man who feels sorry for me,"

she rallied shakily, and found her chin jerked up with ungentle fingers.

"Who feels *what*?" he barked, black eyes glaring forcefully down into the dazed blue of hers. Suddenly his expression changed, and he said softly, "Lady, you don't know what you're saying. Does this seem as if I'm feeling sorry for you?"

His face became a moving blur and then his mouth was warm and hard on hers, moving with a savage kind of tenderness until, sighing, her lips parted under the growing urgency of his kiss. Her hands loosened their grip on his shirt and ran slowly up the taut muscles of his back, pressing him down to her as he folded her into the hard arc of his body.

"Did that seem as if I'm *sorry* for you?" His breath fanned warmly across her ear before his mouth nibbled provocatively at her ear.

"Oh, Burt...."

His head lifted and his eyes had a dangerous glitter about them when he said tersely, "The name is Grant."

"I know," she whispered, brushing his rough-skinned face with her fingertips, "but you seem like two different people to me. There's Burt the thief, and Grant the rancher. I...I don't know which one I...."

He stared down into her eyes for a few hard moments, then swung his head thoughtfully to where Josh stood patiently waiting, whiling away the time by pulling at the sparse grass bunches at the roadside.

"There's only one way I can prove to you that we're one and the same man," he said grimly.

"Come on." He bent suddenly and swung her up into his arms, and in another moment she was seated on Josh's back staring down uncomprehendingly when Grant came back from the car and thrust her handbag at her. "Here, you'd better carry it this time."

The memory of how she had accused him of stealing her wallet sent another wave of agonized guilt through her. How could she have suspected him of petty theft? Even when she had thought him a fugitive, there had been nothing petty about him.

"You weren't to know that I wasn't a purse snatcher," he said at her ear as they moved off up the incline.

"Where are you taking me?" she asked tremulously, but she didn't need his answer. It had been almost dark the last time she had traveled this way with him on Josh's back, but now the sun lightened the green of trees that had seemed oppressive that night, dappling the shade under them with fitful brightness.

Grant's arm tightened around her as suddenly they came upon the clearing, reining Josh to a halt as if he shared Dani's fanciful sense of magic.

And it *was* like an enchanted cottage set away in a never-never land where dreams were the reality. Whatever happened to her in the future, she knew that the tumbledown cabin would always have a special place in her heart.

Yet panic sent a shiver through her when Grant helped her from the horse and held her close to the hard outline of his body, his black eyes searching as they went over her face.

"I'll light a fire," he said huskily. "You're cold."

She wasn't cold in that way, but she forced a smile and nodded, watching him as he led Josh to the lean-to shed before going herself toward the cabin. A tremor shook her again when she put her hand on the door latch, and she stood paralyzed as a new knowledge seeped through to her.

She was inside the cabin when Grant came back, her eyes going around the primitively furnished room as if every piece of ancient furniture were not intimately familiar.

Glancing just once at her bemused face, he strode over to the black stove and busied himself with the making of a fire. It wasn't necessary, she knew, because the room still held the trapped heat of the day, but she needed the time to think.

When Grant turned at last to where she sat at the table, brushing off his hands on his light brown work pants, her eyes met his with a directness he didn't flinch from.

"He lived here, didn't he?" she voiced the question, although there was no doubt in her mind now that this was where her grandfather had centered his reclusive life.

Grant made no prevarication. "Yes," he said simply, watching her closely again for signs of...what? Disappointment? Horror?

But she felt nothing of those things. In the strange way her life had taken lately, she knew that in no other way could she have come to know—and perhaps understand—the grandfather she had never met. The peace and solitude he had found here had been more necessary to him than the call of his distant son.

"He must have loved her very much," she said with a catch in her voice.

Again Grant seemed to know without explanation. "Yes, he did. Life can be pretty unlivable when half of it's gone."

"Did he. . . did he ever talk about her?"

Grant lifted his shoulders in a dismissing shrug. "Not much. But then—" he pulled out the chair opposite and sat down "—neither would I if the wife I loved. . . died."

"What were you doing here?" she asked softly, her eyes misty blue as they went over the face she knew would never be erased from her mind, or her heart. "That day when you. . . rescued me from my car?"

He rubbed a rasping hand over his dark chin and looked at her half sheepishly. "I'd been out for a few days getting the stock to higher land because of the flooding. I'd sent the men back, and I was just doing a last-minute check on the south pasture where I was today. That's how I happened to be there when you went into the ditch."

"And you knew who I was, even then?" There was no accusation in her voice, only the need to tie up all the loose ends flapping around in her mind.

"I guessed," he admitted, "from the license plates on your car, and because. . . ." He paused, then looked around at the stove. "I think we have some coffee left; I'll make some."

A smile curved the soft line of her lips as he busied

himself dipping water and settling the battered coffeepot on the stove. He wasn't going to get away with one thing that she needed to know, not one thing.

"Because?" she prompted when he had to turn back at last and resume his seat.

"Because what?" He pretended bewilderment.

"You guessed who I was because of the license plates and...?"

"Oh. Well, your grandfather had shown me that picture of you when he got it from your mother, and I remembered what you looked like."

Dani rested her chin on one hand and looked at him thoughtfully. "And you kept the memory fresh with that picture by your bed?"

The sudden dark gleam at the back of his eyes, and the smile that stretched his mobile lips over strong white teeth, felt like molten gold in her midriff.

"All right, I'll tell you. I've been in love with you from the minute I saw that picture. After your grandfather died, I found it among his papers and—" a pause "—I'm not ashamed to say that I kept it. Close to where I wanted you to be one day."

"How could you have known that I'd come here as I did?"

He shook his head and reached across the table for her slim-boned hand. "I'd have come down there to find you," he said simply, and Dani knew that it was true. She couldn't imagine anything deterring Grant King from getting something he wanted badly, and he must have wanted her, to have gone to all the subterfuge of pretending to live in this old cabin himself.

"Why didn't you tell me about grandfather right away?"

He shrugged again and ran his thumb disturbingly over her palm. "I couldn't let you get away that soon, and—I didn't want you to think too badly of old Hank. You seemed to be hell-bent on getting all the money you thought he had."

Dani stared at him blankly. "I never wanted money for myself," she said indignantly. "It was for my mother, to pay for the medical treatment she needs."

Grant returned her blank stare; then another, deeper, smile dipped across his mouth. "*That's* why you wanted the ranch? I thought...." His fingers closed on hers in a bone-crushing hold. "Sweetheart, your mother will have all the treatment she needs. I can afford it. And then when she's better, she can come up here and live with us. You said she'd like it here."

"She would, but...." Dani bit softly at her lower lip. "I don't know how she'll take it that...that I want to marry a man I've known for less than two weeks."

"You do want to marry me?"

He asked the question in a stark way that spoke of uncertainty, and Dani turned her palm up to meet his. Could it be that the powerful Grant King was unsure of himself? "You'd better know it," she said huskily, and in another moment she found herself caught up with iron-clad arms, her chin forcibly lifted so her eyes could meet his dangerously glinting ones.

"You're sure?" he demanded roughly, leaving her no room to reply when his head swooped and his mouth imprisoned hers in a hold she knew she would never want to be free of. The whole gamut of emotions pierced her sensitive nerve ends... savagery, tenderness, adoration, and a final urgent demand that went beyond emotions that could be voiced....

Dani struggled back to awareness, to the knowledge that the hard bunk lay under her and Grant's hard weight lay over her. She felt as she had that other time when he had made love to her here, but different in knowing that this would be no short-term love affair. This was forever, for all the days and nights of their togetherness. The name she had first known him by slipped off her tongue, and she felt his immediate withdrawal after a muffled curse.

"Can't you forget Burt?" he gritted through clenched teeth. "He's the one who cheated you, who let you think he was a thief hiding out from the law, who sneaked out the first night you were here and brought living supplies from the ranch. Who didn't make it clear to you that he'd given up law because he wanted to fulfill his boyhood dream of becoming a rancher."

"And your dream's come true, hasn't it?" she said huskily, her fingers roaming familiarly through his thick hair. "You're a rancher, and—" her fingers tautened in his hair "—a man lots of women would love to marry. Myra, for instance."

"Myra?" he echoed disbelievingly, then a laugh rumbled deep in his chest. "She's okay as an office assistant, but she lacks a few things in the wifely stakes." His mouth kissed the pale softness of her cheeks, the hairline of her blond locks. "Like the ability to bake bread on an ancient wood stove, and a strange way of winding her way around my heart."

"But you're still a thief," Dani said dreamily, letting her finger trace the forceful outline of his mouth. "Just the way I always thought you were."

"I've never stolen anything in my life," he said belligerently, raising his head to look with hurt indignation into her eyes.

"You did, my darling Grant," she said softly. "You stole my heart, and that makes you a thief."

Love...

the universal language

**That's why women
all over the world
reach for**

Harlequin Romances

**...from the publisher that
understands the way you feel
about love.**

**Let world-famous authors thrill you
with the joy of love! Be swept to
exotic, faraway places! Delight in
romantic adventure!**

Harlequin Romances
Six brand-new novels every month!

Available at your favorite store or through
Harlequin Reader Service

In U.S.A.
MPO Box 707
Niagara Falls,
NY 14302

In Canada
649 Ontario Street
Stratford,
Ont. N5A 6W2

Harlequin Presents...

The books that let you escape
into the wonderful world of romance!
Trips to exotic places...interesting
plots...meeting memorable people...
the excitement of love....These are
integral parts of Harlequin Presents—
the heartwarming novels read by
women everywhere.

Many early issues are now available.
Choose from this great selection!

Choose from this great selection of exciting Harlequin Presents editions